IN THE STREETZ 3

Tears of War

TRON HILL

URBAN AINT DEAD

URBAN AINT DEAD
P.O Box 448
Maybrook, NY 12543

All rights reserved. Published by URBAN AINT DEAD Publications.

Cover Design: P. Wise / The Wise Services

Edited By: Shawna Brim / Ladies Of Lit

Contact Publisher at www.urbanaintdead.com

Email: urbanaintdead@gmail.com

Print ISBN: 979-8-9906748-4-4

<u>Soundtracks</u>

Scan the QR Code below to listen to the Soundtracks/Singles of some
of your favorite U.A.D titles:

Don't have Spotify or Apple Music?
No Sweat!
Visit your choice streaming platform and search URBAN AINT
DEAD.

Currently on lock serving a bid?
JPay, iHeartRadio, WHATEVER!
We got you covered.

Simply log into your facility's kiosk or tablet, go to music and search
URBAN AINT DEAD.

URBAN AINT DEAD

Like & Follow us on social media:
FB - URBAN AINT DEAD
IG: @urbanaintdead
Tik Tok - @urbanaintdead

<u>**Submissions**</u>

Submit the first three chapters of your completed manuscript to urbanaintdead@gmail.com, subject line: Your book's title. The manuscript must be in a .doc file and sent as an attachment. The document should be in Times New Roman, double-spaced, and in size 12 font. Also, provide your synopsis and full contact information. If sending multiple submissions, they must each be in a separate email. Have a story but no way to submit it electronically? You can still submit to URBAN AINT DEAD. Send in the first three chapters, written or typed, of your completed manuscript to:

URBAN AINT DEAD
P.O Box 448
Maybrook, NY 12543

DO NOT send original manuscript. Must be a duplicate.
Provide your synopsis and a cover letter containing your full contact information.
Thanks for considering URBAN AINT DEAD.

CONTENTS

CHAPTER ONE

"*S*assy..." *he said as he took her into his arms, tightly hugging her, not ever wanting to let her go.*

"Hey, baby." She smiled beautifully, caressing the back of his head with her heavenly hands. Her body was soft as feathers, just like he remembered it. Her smell was an aroma of blissfulness.

Everything about her appearance was in its proper place, except for one thing — he had forgotten about it until now. It was only then that he noticed her stomach was absent of any signs of pregnancy. He didn't want to think about it.

It took a few minutes for him to release her. He was afraid that he'd lose her a second time.

Why? he asked himself. A tear ebbed from the web of his eye. Ace had been partially amazed that he could feel it slide down his face. It was strange how she sensed what laid within him.

"It's okay, baby. I'll never leave you."

Slightly, he pulled away from her grasp, admiring the face of his beautiful life. Damn, she's so pretty, he thought.

She lifted a hand to his cheek, removing the small, glistening stream. "How have you been?" Sassy smiled. Her white teeth sparkled with every word.

"Not good. Nothing is good without you." Ace dropped his head toward the ground, ashamed that he hadn't protected her — angry that he'd failed her.

"Ace, I'm still here with you, baby." Sassy placed a hand on his chest, exactly over his heart, a place which her presence would never leave. Ever.

"I know…" he finally got out, giving a half smile. "But everything's so different without…"

"Shhh…" She lifted her index finger to his lips. "Ace, I know how you feel. But baby, you can't let what happened stop you from living. Ace, you have to live for both of us."

"I ca-can't," he stuttered. "It's-it's hard. I love you too much…" His words trailed off. Tears formed multiple rivers down his face. They were out of his control.

"I love you too much, Ace. And if you really love me, then live… and always trust and believe that I'm always with you. Forever more."

Ace took her hands within his, lifted them to his face, and kissed her palms passionately. Her hands were the sweetest things his lips had tasted in a long time.

Gazing down at her physique, he desperately wanted to do the same to all of her. Then, he noticed the inevitable.

"Sassy! Sassy!!!" Ace yelled out in panic. He watched helplessly as she began to fade away. "Sassy, baby, please don't leave me," he pleaded, continuing to watch her vanish into thin air.

"I love you, Ace." Those were the last words he heard her say.

"Sassy!!!" he screamed out. Nothing came in return besides that of his very own echo. Miserably, he collapsed to his knees, releasing all of the tormenting agony which had built up inside of him for so long.

He didn't know how to forgive himself for letting her death happen. For letting Black win. Surely, he was smiling somewhere down in hell at the wretched person he'd left on Earth. He was probably still happy by the fact of knowing that he'd taken the most important part of his existence.

"How am I supposed to live? How?!!!" he yelled just before the sounds of a piano began resonating in the depths of his ears. Ace *turned and realized that he now stood in a part of the past he hated so much. It was the funeral of his life, soul, and heart.*

Regretfully, Ace stepped slowly up the aisle, bypassing old friends — and the family of the dearly departed. As he continued to move toward the closed, mahogany casket, he wished he wasn't here. He wished he couldn't relive this part of his memory.

People sat on both sides, mourning the loss of life, unaware of his presence, even while he moved by. Nothing had changed about it. These were the same woeful expressions.

Finally making it to the front, his body became rigid. His eyes were now fixated on the radiant casket before him. The last thing he wanted to do was lift the lid and be forced to witness her lifeless body again — though a burning urge compelled him to do so.

His fingers latched onto the edge of the seal...

From somewhere behind him, he heard a woman's loud shriek. It was exactly the same as last time.

Reluctantly, Ace eased it upward. Instantly, a shallow gasp escaped him as his mouth fell open at the sight before his eyes. It wasn't her. It was him. He continued to stare in confusion, disbelief. His heart pounded harder and faster against the walls of his chest, as if it were ready to make an exit.

Something had either clogged his windpipe or the oxygen had faded into inexistence in mere seconds. He couldn't breathe, and his lungs were beginning to cry for air.

Then — just like before — the woman continued to sob, yelling, "You bastard... You the reason..."

Ace didn't have to see who had said it because he already knew. However, something other than himself had swiveled him around against his own free will.

It was Sassy's mother. Her face was puffed with rage; nonetheless, she was a beautiful reflection of her daughter. She stood with her tears running wildly down her face. "You deserved that, not my precious baby." She continued to repeat her words before pulling out a chrome revolver from her purse. Without hesitation, she took aim at his chest.

Badly, he wanted to spin away from its marker, but a force was holding him in place. His gaze trailed the length of the barrel.

"You bastard, you deserve it," she barked again before firing.

"AGGHHH!!!" HE GROWLED AS HE CAME FROM HIS SLUMBER. ACE'S hands ran over the skin of his chest in search for the hole he expected to feel. But it wasn't real. Only the scars which were left by Black.

How many times had this dream occurred? He'd lost count somewhere after the hundredth time. They'd been a constant reminder of Sassy's death.

Ace sat up in bed, rubbing over his healed wounds, pondering about how bad his life was. He'd survived when he wanted nothing more than to die as a sacrifice for the love of his life. *Damn, why had the opposite occurred?*

It was a little past a year now since that unforgettable night took place which branded every single detail of the event into his memory. He'd never forget, regardless of the lapse of time.

The world he loved was shattered. A bullet had grazed his skull, while a second one penetrated the flesh of his torso. One left him to suffer the worst kind of migraines. The other left an empty hole in his life — both symbols of failure. As well, both were a constant reminder of the person he'd let down.

Ace swept his eyes around the dark interior of the room which he'd transformed into a prison cell. Day after day, this had become his only dwelling place. So, reclusive he became. He avoided the free world as if it were an anathema. All of which led his persona to match that of a hermit. Secluded away from everything besides his thoughts — and sometimes Whiteboy. Both — at times — could be more than annoying and appreciated. They kept him… existent. And without them, he more than likely would have ended it all. Like everything he cared about.

Finally getting up from the bed, Ace stared down at his feet. Then, he glanced around at the living quarters he was used to. It was a clustered, small area with piles of clothes and all types of other things scattered about.

Damn, it looked so — trashy. He now wondered how long it had been in this condition. But why did he care now? He hadn't cared before, and obviously, neither did Whiteboy.

Stepping out into the hallway, Ace quickly noticed that the apartment was a *very* different environment. He wiped at his eyes to make sure he was seeing it correctly. The scenery was almost spotless. Evidently, Whiteboy was domesticated as fuck.

Ace began to question exactly how long he'd been cooped up in the room. This sight was definitely something he'd missed days — well, months before.

He walked into the living room where the TV was playing. At first, he paid it no mind. The apartment still held him in awe. There sat a new living room set, drowned in a burgundy hue with two side tables to match. The big ass TV sat opposite of that with some type of exotic painting hanging above it. The art was a naked, beautiful African female, partially covered by a single rose petal. Two video games systems and games were scattered underneath.

Ace turned his head toward the kitchen and spotted a sleek, black, Italian table surrounded by matching stools. The set complimented the space, exuding an alluring taste.

Moments later, the words from the television pierced his ears. *"Niggas be doing shit, and then when the shit comes back to them — karma — they be wanting niggas to have sympathy and feel sorry for 'em while they become another person's burden cause they on some handicap shit..."*

Moving toward the TV, Ace stared at the light-skinned, chubby faced guy who was the one doing the talking.

Who the fuck is this nigga talking bout? Ace asked himself as though the guy had been actually referring to him. Surely, he was no one's burden. Yet then again, hadn't Whiteboy been taking care of him since his release from the hospital and the police's custody?

Keeping his retinas focused on the guy, he wondered how he'd feel if a nigga gunned him down and took that diamond cut medallion from around his neck that said, "A.M. Trigga." The name located at the bottom of the screen said the same.

At first sight, you'd think the man was some type of rapper or another arrogant ass nigga who loved to hear himself talk. But he was surrounded by a group of individuals who listened as if he was a professor giving vital information on their course.

And now, he had Ace's attention on the lecture as well.

"*I mean,*" the guy said, glancing around at all the curious stares, "*I see niggas everyday get fucked up or put in fucked up situations where they lose something or somebody. And then, they become them same handicaps I was just talking about.*

"*They make excuses, blaming everything they can think of for what happened to them. They use this as their reason for not doing what they could — or need to — do. Just on some real shit, nigga, you in the position you in because you want to be. That's just what it is.*

"*It's like this. It's not about what the fuck happened. Fuck what happened, nigga. This shit is about what you do after whatever has happened. Shawty, my pops got shot in the face and it caused him to go blind for the rest of his life...*"

He paused, taking a deep gulp from the water bottle he'd picked up from somewhere. "*Now, he easily could of balled up in a fetal position and ended up being one of those same handicaps. But hell nah. Nigga, he sucked that shit up and got back on his grind even harder — and he still going hard. I see that as some real nigga shit, period. I got a motto I tell people all the time...*" He pointed around the space aimlessly at those who occupied it.

"*It's my wrongdoing, in my doing of nothing. Meaning, I'm wrong if Trigga is doing nothing to change any situation I don't like now — or in the future. And if I don't change it, then I deserve every bit of what I'm getting.*"

The screen began to fade away with the chatter of a few applauders. Then, a few bullet holes, complimented with the sound effects of gunfire, came onto the screen.

The abrupt noise caused Ace to jump a little. It was not necessarily because of the sound itself but due to its suddenness when he was still caught up on dude's words.

Fo sho he had uttered some real talk, talk that Ace felt he needed to hear.

Leaving the TV to change programs, he pivoted, heading for the bathroom with the phrase, *"my wrongdoing is my doing of nothing,"* ringing loudly in his head.

The idiom was catchy, he had to admit. Ace wasn't the type of person to dick ride a nigga. Hell, he was too caught up on his own dick, which left no room for others in his thinking process. But this A.M. Trigga character gave him something to always remember.

After turning on the hot water in the shower, Ace had opened the pantry's door when he caught a disturbing glimpse of his reflection.

"Damn, Ace…" he uttered sotto voce, unable to advert his gaze. In his opinion, the image fit the description of a deranged, mentally ill patient.

A fucking handicap. He grimaced at the thought. The flesh encircling his eyes was a purplish hue and puffy. His skin complexion was that of an ashen corpse. His hair looked as if it hadn't been brushed in years. Yet, the left side appeared to be *sort* of okay. And that was only because a patch of hair was missing from that particular side. It had been the result of Black's bullet which grazed his skull.

The memento angered him. "I should of killed you first," he whispered, rubbing over one of his scars of defeat. Ace hated the fact that it wasn't him who'd planted the slug in him.

Whiteboy told him how it all went down after he collapsed. Black had unloaded on him, hitting Sassy in the process. Then, he had sprang into the room a little too late, chopping down the last person standing.

Of course he was grateful, but damn, why couldn't he have been a few seconds sooner? Though on the same token, why had *he* insisted that Whiteboy wait for something he sort of felt wouldn't be possible?

At the end of the day, he could only blame himself. His best friend had followed his orders, like loyal niggas were supposed to do.

The vapors from the steaming shower covered the mirror, causing Ace to finally veer away from the unsettling image. He now regretted letting himself fall to such an extent. Ace knew he had to do something fast or continue to be wrong for doing nothing.

Staring up at the ceiling, his mind went back to the dream of Sassy and her words. *You have to live for both of us…* He hadn't for a year and counting. However, today would be the beginning of *their* new life.

"I'ma live for us both, baby. I love you, Sassy," he uttered toward the ceiling before stepping into the shower, anxious to finally wash away months of his stale self. It was time to.

AN HOUR LATER, ACE WALKED BACK INTO HIS *CELL*, LOOKING AROUND for something to put on, yet he saw nothing to reflect how he was feeling. Damn near all of his clothes were wrinkled up in piles. Some were still dirty from days ago. And some, months ago.

Knowing there would be nothing of use at this very moment, he turned and headed for Whiteboy's domain.

Immediately, Ace noticed that his room matched the rest of the apartment. Spotless.

Ain't no fucking way I'm the only one here living like a fucking bum —_a fucking handicap, Ace thought jokingly, but nonetheless, he was aware of its truthfulness.

He pulled open the closet door, instantly finding a pile of fabrics at the foot of the threshold. "Fronting ass nigga…" He laughed, kicking the top of the pile to the side as he moved by, going straight for the dry cleaned clothes hanging up.

After a few seconds of inventory checking, he found the perfect fit for how he was feeling. Without hesitation, he removed a pair of Foreign Republik jeans from under the plastic covering then stepped out to try them on. He and Whiteboy had been the same size, but due to his depressing state, he could now tell he'd drastically fallen off.

"A belt will have to do for the time being," he said to himself, staring at how loosely the pants were at his waist. Going back into the closet, he fished out the Foreign Republik t-shirt with a red negative, outlined print of the Statue of Liberty on the back. *Arrogant and Ridiculous* was stamped in a half circle on the front, matching the hue of the back.

The shirt definitely matched the old Ace to the tee and likewise, would the new. Sliding his arms into the sleeves, he stared down at himself, thinking that now all he needed was a nice pair of shoes to finish it off.

Luckily for him, they also wore close to the same size in shoes. He shoved the clothes to the side and saw a few pairs of sneakers, but none of which could be rocked with the fit.

"Fuck. I'ma grab some today," he told himself, snatching up the pair of white and burgundy Nike Air Max.

His ears caught the sound of keys hitting against the front door. Whiteboy.

This nigga gonna be mad I'm in his shit, but so the fuck what? He smiled, making his way toward the front as Whiteboy came in.

Whiteboy's first expression seemed as if he'd stumbled upon a ghost. His shock quickly transformed into gladness. "I know that ain't my muthafucking nigga, Ace!" he exuberantly let out.

Ace couldn't help but to smile in return at his brother who, quite obviously, was happy to see him up and about. At last. "The one and muthafucking only," he shot back.

Whiteboy was glad he'd bounced back from his stupor. It had been a minute *too* long since he'd seen him so full of life. "About fucking time yo handicap ass came out of that dungeon." He laughed, unaware of the wince Ace gave at the mentioning of the word *handicap*.

"Nigga, ain't shit handicap," Ace snapped in return, wondering how many times he would hear the word today.

"Now…" Whiteboy joked, reaching out to dap him up. They brotherly embraced one another as if they hadn't seen each other in years. Though this had been a long-awaited reunion.

"What you got right there?" Ace asked, eyeing the bags curiously after Whiteboy sat them on the table.

"Shid, some tofu. I figured you'd probably be hungry in a few more days." He chuckled, playfully punching at his shoulder.

"Man, hell yeah. I most definitely got to get my weight back. Nigga round this bitch small as fuck," he said, showing him the extra space in the pants.

"Nah, I probably need to slow down." Whiteboy laughed, patting his stomach.

Finishing off the food, they didn't waste another minute on catching up on lost time. Whiteboy filled him in on everything he'd been doing to make sure they were straight and all that had taken place in the streets.

Ace had to admit that he missed the streets, and his best friend told him the feeling was mutual because the streets missed him as well. With him out of the streets, his team was barely above water. And they weren't even sticking together anymore, just doing their own thing, hitting each other every so often when they were near the hood.

Though Ariel was still staying close to Whiteboy's side, patiently waiting for Ace to make his predestined return. Her and Whiteboy had been executing a few moves together, here and there, when she wasn't messing with the white-collar game.

Dre would get at Whiteboy two to three times a week. He wasn't fooling around with the robbing shit though. He was still selling dope out of a little spot off of Memorial Drive. It was nothing close to what he used to make yet enough to make ends meet.

Then, there was Kero and Lil Spain, who were doing something close, but it was not the same numbers they once did with Ace. Somehow, they were bringing in more than the rest of them. Whiteboy was at first suspicious of it, but he soon found out that they'd hit a sweet lick and took off from there. Whenever they ran into Whiteboy, they always told him that if Ace needed anything, they were only a call away. And Whiteboy held them to their word.

Ace listened attentively, feeling like he'd let them all down by giving in wholeheartedly to the emotions of sadness, grief, and depression, causing all of their futures to fade slowly into nothing.

He shook his head shamefully, understanding the depth of his wrongness and all it would take to remedy it. He was back.

"So, what you got lined up now?" he questioned curiously. The time had come for him to get his feet wet.

Whiteboy stared at him a second then realized his best friend — his brother — was back. His smile broadened. "Some nice shit me and this nigga, Trigga be…"

"Who?" Ace interrupted, caught off guard by the mentioning of another individual. Since he'd remembered, they only worked with the team — no outside niggas. *How much have things changed?*

"Trigga. He from the hood. I hooked up wit him about a month ago. Shawty been pulling all types of moves. Like real nice moves involving a lot of paper. You know…"

Ace cut in again. "And?" He said it as if there was more to it.

"And what?" Whiteboy replied smartly with a raised eyebrow. He knew how Ace would react to the revelation — in the same exact manner. But they were barely eating, so his feelings mattered less at this point. "Anyway, bra eating real good, and right now, he recruiting…"

"Bra, what the fuck I look like? I ain't joining no nigga."

"Nigga, me either." Whiteboy wanted to laugh because he threw that in to fuck with his brother. "But I pushed up on 'em. So, we been talking, and he on some he want to see how niggas work, then we'll go from there. Shid, I mean, I had to link up wit somebody. You disappeared…"

Even though they stayed in the same place, Ace clearly understood what he meant without him having to say more. And he respected the little shot it implicated.

All Ace could say was, "That's what's up."

His calm demeanor made Whiteboy feel sort of awkward, whereas he began to massage his own neck. "We can holla at dude later though. Today, we gone pull up on the boy, Tone. We…"

"Tone?" Ace quickly asked upon hearing the name he hadn't heard in years. "I know you ain't talking bout Tone from Reynolds Town?"

"That's exactly who I'm talking bout. What, you don't fuck wit 'em or some'n?"

"Man, hell nawl. Me and Bl…" He stopped himself from uttering the name.

Whiteboy's eyebrows furrowed in confusion. He thought he knew where he was headed. "Man, Ace, look. Forget whatever y'all had going on. Holme been fucking wit me. Shid, he another one of those reasons we still managing. So, let's just get this paper and take back over the streets," Whiteboy finished with a serious look.

Ace twisted his lips, deciding to respect his best friend's wishes. "I'm game."

Whiteboy nodded his head like that was exactly what he needed to hear. "Good."

"And by the way," Ace stood from the table, "what's the name of the shit the nigga, Trigga, running?"

Whiteboy gazed up at him, smiling. "The Runt'z..."

CHAPTER TWO

Edgewood looked foreign to Ace as they drove along the small streets he grew up in.

The Bricks, which they called the apartments of the neighborhood, had been torn down, leaving only a few houses in different parts of the hood, causing it to seem more like some part of a small country town than a project of Atlanta.

They passed the Red Store, which was now painted yellow. So, he guessed it was the Yellow Store now. A few local jays lingered on the sidewalk with nothing better to do than watch passers fly by their zoned out glares. The hood might not have looked as he remembered it, yet it felt the same. It had been a minute since his face was on the scene, and he knew what would be on niggas' minds once they saw him. But who cared?

Making a right at the stop sign, they parked behind a Ford pickup that two dudes were running a detail business off of. This was Benny Harper's yard, the one spot in the hood which stayed popping due to the liquor served out the back door and the gambling that took place in the grassless back yard. Both things were daily activities, yet they were off the meter when the weekend hit.

"Let me see where this fool at…" Ace heard Whiteboy say while he gazed down the sidewalk at a few local women and men who stood around. Everyone had an idle conversation going with some laughing and drinking, as if there was nothing in the world better to do than to be at Benny's.

Shit never change, he thought, sweeping his eyes over the faces of the yard. People he remembered sat at different tables, playing cards, while another group was gambling on the hood of an old pickup truck — one which hadn't moved since before the last time he saw it.

A short distance away, opposite of those at the pickup, a group of around ten to fifteen people shot dice up against the house on a slab of concrete adjacent to it.

The scenery had always been the same, and depending on who downed too many drinks by the end of the evening, they would be the story of tomorrow.

It never failed. He smirked, sort of missing his old stomping ground.

"Yo, what's good, bra?" Whiteboy asked into his phone, staring aimlessly out the driver's side window. "Yeah… Shid, I'm round the way now," he was saying when Ace decided to step out.

"Say, I'm bout to grab some'n to drink. Want some'n?"

Whiteboy shook his head *no*.

Ace treaded down the walkway, ready to witness some of the funny expressions he knew he was bound to receive once people recognized who moved amongst them.

How could he be mistaken as anyone else? Niggas all over the hood knew his face almost like the back of their hands, and likewise, they'd heard most of the rumors about the situation which took place between him and his former boss/nemesis. He smiled because this was also one of the most frequented spots for a lot of *Black's Hand*. And they were here —_and so was his Ruger .45.

Though Ace tried to remind himself that he wasn't here for beef, he knew it wouldn't hurt to be prepared. Like Drake said, "Being humble don't work as well as being aware."

Faster than he intended, the eyes laid on him. They were those of old comrades, friends, and enemies from the other side. They stared at him unbelievingly, as if a ghost was approaching.

He continued to smirk, badly wanting to say to all, "Yeah, mutha-fuckas, I'm back in this bitch. What!"

Closely, he scrutinized everyone's movement in his sight, watching for any forms of panic or anything that could equate to being a threat.

He watched everything carefully as he'd started out, pretending to walk unmindfully. The last thing he wanted to do was to reveal to niggas how on point he was. That surely would place him at a disad-vantage, especially if someone actually had drama on their mind.

Continuing on, he watched a few people nod their heads as if to replace saying the words, "What up," while the majority offered cold stares as a way of substituting what they really had in mind.

Hell, even the group shooting dice had put him within their scopes whenever the dice allowed them a moment to do so.

Finally stepping up to the back door, Ace glanced around with a smile before knocking twice. A few seconds passed before a bummed-out female appeared in the doorway. She had to be either the old man's worker or slut. Most likely both.

"Say…" Ace began, becoming very conscious of everything moving in his peripheral. "Let me get a cup of Hennessy and a Coke."

"Okay, baby," she replied, revealing her hideous grill as she gladly took the money and disappeared.

Feeling the urge to glance around again, Ace noticed some individuals adverting their gazes away from him yet not enough of them. His attention locked on two dudes who were gambling on the hood of the truck. They were whispering to one another, looking in his direction. It didn't take a rocket scientist to know that they were talking about him.

Talk is all it better be, he thought. The minute he felt it might turn into something else, he'd waste no time in planting bullets in both of them faster than a farmer could drop a seed in the ground.

These muthafuckas knew him though. They weren't stupid. Maybe a little death struck but not stupid. His reputation kept all aware and in check.

Ace swiveled toward the door upon hearing footsteps. The lady returned, handing him his request.

"Damn, stranger, long time no see…" The female's voice came from behind him.

Ace turned to see one of the blackest and sexiest things to walk the streets of the hood. But nonetheless, she was a hoodrat. "What's good, girl?" He smiled at Michelle, who returned one. It had been a good little minute since he'd seen her. He noticed she still possessed every aspect he remembered about her —_her Coke bottle shape and apple shaped ass.

He had to give her physique another look over, which caused her to blush from the attention.

"Nothing much. How have you been?" she exclaimed with a tad of concern riding her voice as if she really cared.

"I've been good and you?"

"Well, you know me. Waiting on my moment." She chuckled.

Bitch, please. You been 'waiting' on that for how long now? was what he wanted to say but thought better than to rain on her parade. "Shid, I hear that…" he retorted, now remembering that the last time he'd heard, she was messing around with a big money nigga from the hood named Richie. Trust and believe, he lived up to every bit of the name. "But I heard you had it."

She placed her hands on her hips, eyeing him curiously with a fake smile. "Boy, you heard wrong."

He smiled, knowing this was the part when bitches began to get amnesia. "Wasn't you fucking wit the boy, Richie?"

She smacked her teeth as if the name disgusted her. "I left that sorry ass nigga. His broke ass ain't talking bout shit…"

Nah, ho, that nigga probably fucked you till he got tired and dropped yo sorry ass. He smiled again, seeing through the fronting she displayed. This was a typical ho, so he expected nothing less than typical ho shit to fall from her lips.

"Damn…" he said, barely managing to keep from laughing in her face.

Michelle reached and rubbed his arm in a caressing manner. "But anyway, you been okay though? I heard what happened."

"I'm good," Ace said, quickly cutting her off, not wanting to go down that road. He guessed she sensed it by the new expression she was giving him.

"Oh, okay, that's what's up. So, who…" Before she had the chance to inquire, Whiteboy called his name.

Instantly, Ace became grateful. His best friend saved him from another road he didn't want to travel down. However, he made a mental note to keep her in mind. She would be a real good ear to the happenings of hood affairs and a good informant on her best man, Richie. At this point, anybody could be their come up.

"Say, I'ma get at you, aight?" he said, giving her a wink afterwards to let her know she was successful on her pitch.

"Okay… do that." She smiled seductively.

Walking toward Whiteboy, Ace immediately caught sight of a few guys moving awkwardly — as if they were trying to get out the way of something or someone. They weren't scrambling but definitely dispersing with a purpose.

Ace's street instincts kicked in, and his guard went on alert as he continued to walk nonchalantly, popping open the Coke. He poured a little bit into his cup of Hennessy, gradually letting his eyes roam in different directions in hopes of seeing the motive for the strange reactions. He saw none, only Whiteboy standing next to a midsize, not fat but chubby dude. The guy was a mixture of brown and red complexions, medium built, with wavy hair and a lot more tattoos than Ace had acquired.

Ace couldn't see the color of his eyes due to the dark Ray-Ban shades he had on. He could also see the pistol hanging out of his pocket.

Making his way across the street, he realized that he might have been the incentive behind the weird occurrence.

He must got the press down on these niggas, Ace thought, reaching the two of them.

"This my brother, Ace, I was telling you about…" said Whiteboy, introducing the two. "Ace," Whiteboy smirked, nodding his head in the guy's direction, "this Trigga."

"What's poppin?" Trigga greeted, letting his face stray toward him then back over the scenery.

"What's good?" Ace returned. He noticed quickly that dude's head wouldn't stay still. Was he paranoid? Probably but his demeanor was a little too calm. A little too in control of himself to be the paranoid type.

He kept his hands collapsed, one on top of the other, like the Mafia, and he spoke coolly as though his words flowed with a rhythm.

"So, what the move is?" Whiteboy asked. Ace raised an eyebrow, observing the change in White's character. He seemed to be vibing off this guy's aura. Hopefully Ace was just tripping.

Ace glanced down into his cup, wondering had he taken too big of a sip.

"Shid, you already know we bout to eat like kings do." Trigga smiled a Colgate smile and continued. "Aye, let's get in the AC and spin the block one time."

Ace watched him swiftly hop into the car then gave Whiteboy an inquisitive look. He smiled slightly in return before getting in. It didn't take long for Ace to know he'd gotten into a rental. The smell told it all. These were every street dude's preference of whips to drive when conducting business. Well, if they possessed any common sense.

Ace tossed the remainder of the Coke and followed suit. As they pulled away, Whiteboy asked, "You wanna blow one?" He took out some Kush from his pocket.

"Nah, ion blow while doing b.i."

Ace stared at the back of Trigga's head funnily as if to say, "This nigga is full of himself."

"Aight, look right, this how we finna play the situation. You and Dawg..." he began, adjusting his rearview mirror but obviously speaking to Whiteboy. "Gonna go in and go the fuck crazy. Not on no killing people shit but making sure they get the point and move as told. A nigga shouldn't have to tell you how to handle your part, so just be quick and effective. Me and ya boy..." he said, indicating Ace with a nod. He then pulled his shades down, so they could see eye to eye in the rearview. "We gone be right behind y'all. And Ace, as soon as we hit the door, go straight for the cases. Don't be picky bout which ones to pop. We want all we can get and more. I been laying on this for a minute, so I know whatever we grab is good. Just pop and scoop as fast as you can. I'ma take the left and leave the right to you, aight?"

Ace nodded, feeling like he dressed it up to sound a lot less than what it was. Nothing was that simple, especially a heist. Though at the same time, he hoped it would be for Trigga's sake.

Trigga turned his attention back to White. "Whiteboy, I haven't seen you work. But niggas talk, and real shit, I want to see what I've been hearing in HD. And shawty," he took a quick glance at Ace, "I already know how you get down. But you been sleep for a minute. Don't let that be an inconvenience. Sleepers get left." He removed the Ray-Bans from his face as a way of letting Ace see his seriousness.

Clearly, he understood what *left* insinuated, and he definitely wasn't eligible for that. Ace felt a slight urge to laugh at the mild threat. "So, what, we going in skied up?"

Trigga let out a chuckle. "We don't do the ski mask shit. That's for amateurs. We the fitted cap boys."

Ace began to think. Either Trigga was very good at what he did or flat out crazy to be running up in a spot with some fucking hat on. And by the way, he didn't even know what they had in mind as the lick. He could only tell that it had to be some residential shop which meant one thing: cameras.

Pulling back up at Benny Harper's yard, Trigga spoke yet again, stopping Ace from getting out. "Say, my nigga..." He turned around toward him. "I know what I'm doing. So just trust me and do what I say."

"Yeah... Aight," Ace flatly returned, wondering if he knew how to read minds too.

As him and Whiteboy headed back toward their rental, he noticed Michelle. She noticed him as well, eyeing him down like she'd been religiously waiting.

He smiled, realizing how thirsty she was to fall victim to his bullshit. "Aye…" he called out, getting Whiteboy's attention. "Let's chill a sec, aight?"

Seeing what his gaze had locked upon, Whiteboy smiled. "I'ma be in the car. Man, don't be all day. We still got other shit to do," he reminded him.

"What's good, Michelle?" he uttered jokingly, motioning her closer.

"You tell me, Ace."

Yeah, she too ready, he thought. "That's what I'm trying to figure out right now."

"I'm wit whatever you wit… And a little more," she told him sexually, letting her eyes trail his physique as he leaned against the front of the vehicle.

"Oh, yeah? We'll definitely see." He smiled, glancing around the live scenery. "So, be honest with me. You and that nigga, Richie, done on some real shit?" He returned a lustrous expression, truly admiring her curves. It was part of the game, but his dick began to harden at the view.

"Boy, hell yeah. That nothing ass nigga ain't talking about shit. He don't wanna do nothing but fuck all day with that lil bitty ass dick and front like he got it all. He ain't got money like niggas think. His lame ass," she finished with a disgusted look.

"Really? Girl, I can't go for that. Shawty definitely caked up," Ace assured her as if he was for certain. He knew all he had to do to get a ho talking was to contradict what she thought she knew. That would make them talk for days.

"He got a little something, yes. But not what people think. I only seen him with *a lot* of cash one time, and I mean a lot*.*" She added emphasis to stress exactly what she meant by *a lot*. "And that was only because he'd ripped off some country boys and ain't have nowhere to put it besides in the house…"

"Oh…" Ace interrupted, a little more interested. "You were staying with 'em?"

"Of course…" Her eyebrows furrowed as if the question offended her somewhat. "I was his bitch, not one of these lil ratchet hos. Boy, stop! Got me bent if a ni…"

Someone interrupted her, calling Ace's name. And after catching another look of disgust written across Michelle's face, he craned his neck backwards to see a dirty ass, frail zombie coming his way.

D-nice? Couldn't be. He stared in all out disbelief. The only way he came to the conclusion of it actually being D-nice was due to his facial features and that unmistakable smile. Yet the golds were no longer how he remembered. They looked dull and like they were slowly deteriorating right along with his body. His clothes seemed to be straight out of the sewers. His old protégé's situation looked miserable.

"Nice?" he finally got out, making sure it was him but hoping like hell it wasn't though.

"What's up, big bra?" D-nice said, confirming something he didn't want to believe. He stuck his damaged hand out for some dap.

"What up…" Ace returned appallingly, half-heartedly dapping him up. He refused to feel sorry for him, remembering what he'd done. However, that wouldn't prevent him from feeling like *damn!* "Man, I heard bout what happened. And man, I wanna apologize for…"

"Shawty, I don't need your sorries. The shit is what it is," Ace shot at him. Damn, he didn't need the whole fucking world bringing the shit up with all the fake sympathy.

"I… I feel ya, man. Ace, shit been real bad for a nigga and…" D-nice was cut off a second time. This time, it was not because of Ace but due to the sound of a car horn blaring.

Ace glanced over at Whiteboy, who was signaling the time had come to pull. "Here…" he said, handing D-nice the rest of his liquor. He then turned his attention back to Michelle, whose face said she wasn't ready to part ways.

"Say, bae. Put ya math in the phone. I'ma hit you later," he told her, fishing his phone out and handing it to her.

"Mann!" Michelle began, sounding like a disappointed child. "I guess later is better than never. And you betta call me too." She seductively licked her lips, exhibiting what she had in mind.

This bitch dumb thirsty. He smirked, thinking her mouth would be something extra to go with the intel she'd willingly give to him on

Richie. "Man, you gots to know I'm fucking wit you," he assured, getting a handful of her soft ass, tugging her closer.

"We'll see." She wanted him to do more than just grab her ass.

"Where to?" he asked Whiteboy immediately after hopping in, needing to put something else on his mind. He had to calm his dick down. It had been some time since he hit some pussy, and that little, soft ass did nothing but excite him —_way more than he thought it would or intended.

"We finna go holla at this nigga, Tone." Whiteboy smiled, putting the vehicle into gear.

"What's good, lil mama? You leaving wit a nigga or what?" Q asked the fine ass dime piece he'd been caked up with all night in Platinum Twenty One. He may not have had the looks to bag fine bitches of this particular one's caliber, but his money could grab a million of them. Which most likely was the sole reason she'd been under his arm a majority of the night.

He'd caught her seductive glances a few times at the bar, and after being allowed an entire view of her unique physique, he became determined to leave with her. To him, she possessed too much femininity for some of these lames in the club, who were fake putting on as if they were made, when they didn't even own a pot to piss in.

Quite obviously, they weren't her type. She only got with the real bankers. The big boys.

"That depends on where we headed..." She sexually teased him, sliding her tongue across the surface of her glossed upper lip. That caused his dick to jerk as if it wanted some of that attention.

"Shid, baby, we can go to the moon if you like."

She giggled flirtatiously. "Nigga, I hope you got a pilot's license."

"What? Yen know..." he responded, retrieving a knot of crisped bills from his pocket.

The female became moon eyed, staring at the bank roll, amazed by its size. Her pussy got wetter. She wondered how deep this nigga's pockets really went and was more than willing to find out. "Damn,

Captain…" She got a palm full of his crotch without hesitation, applying a passionate massage with her grasp. Her nose brushed against the flesh of his neck.

"Mmm…" vibrated from his throat. Q bit down on his bottom lip, ready for whatever she intended on offering.

He lifted her chin to his. His dick was beginning to harden, wanting to explore the inside of her sea. "We can dip set now…" he told her, seeing no reason in continuing to procrastinate. She'd given him the *right away*, and now, it was time to go.

Uttering a few words, Q dapped a couple of guys as they made their way toward the exit. He wondered why lil mama, who he led by hand, seemed to be avoiding face-to-face contact with a few of his people that were trying to check out the catch of the night.

She probably don't want to appear as some rip. Or she probably done fucked one or two of these niggas before, he thought, brushing off the odd actions as something minor. If she had fucked one of them or more, it was nothing. Fo sho he would be an add on to her roster.

Yeah, this nigga caked, the female mused, glancing over the 2022 BMW XM AWD he was pushing.

He noticed her astonished reaction. "Niggas ain't fucking with this muthafucka," he boasted arrogantly with a haughty smile. Very few people in the city could purchase one of them.

"It's… exotic," she returned, not wanting to sound *too* groupie-ish or enlarge his head bigger than it already was.

"Nah, it's German…" He chuckled, disabling the alarm system and unlocking the doors, so they could get in. "Aye, we can go get some'n to eat after we blow this. Then I guess grab a spot to go chill at." He smiled, reaching down into the console, retrieving a sandwich bag of weed.

"I guess…" She smirked, inspecting the contents of the bag before parting the seal. "Oh… damn." She immediately jerked her head backwards from the strong aroma which attacked her nostrils. "What the fuck is this?" she asked with a wrinkled face.

Q laughed. "That's that Alaska Thunder Fuck… Straight outta Compton."

"Is it safe? That's all I wanna know." The female chuckled, pinching off a ball of the sticky bud. "You got wraps?"

"Nope. I'm old school wit it." Q pulled down the sun visor, letting a pack of 20/20 rolling papers fall into his lap.

"Whaaat?" She laughed, shocked. "My type of nigga."

"Girl, like you fuck wit 'em?"

"Nigga, who? I been on these since high school." She gestured with her hand as if to show her old height.

"Well, we finna see what ya smoke game like then. All that fronting," he said, watching her carefully roll up the piff. Her lips were so sexy and pretty that he couldn't help but to become even more aroused. He fixated on the way she put it between her lips, twisting, licking, and sliding it from side to side.

She began to grin upon noticing that she'd grasped his full attention. Her actions were on purpose, especially having forethought of the ending result.

"I wanna show you a trick," she told him, grabbing the lighter from the cup holder. "Let me see it…" Her eyes dropped to his crotch.

He didn't quite know what she had in mind but was glad, especially after following the direction of her gaze. He tried his best to be nonchalant about it though couldn't help his fast ass hands as they undid his pants, revealing the fully erect manhood.

Oookkkaaayy, little man. She wanted to laugh badly at the inside joke. Nine times out of ten, if a nigga was popping big shit, he had nothing more than *lil* shit between his legs. That was very true at this moment. She smiled. Firing up the gas, she took a quick pull. "Smoke…" She put the joint to his lips. She then picked up the cup of Grey Goose and pineapple she'd brought along. Taking a gulp, she held most of the liquor in her mouth, set the cup down, and maneuvered her body into a position where her knees were now on the seat with her face lingering over him.

Aight, bitch, let's see how fye you is, Q thought, taking another drag of the gas. He now realized what she had in mind and was praying she'd execute it like a vet. Because if not, she'd be sucking until his boxers and pants were dry.

Placing her lips at the tip of the head, she wanted to laugh, thinking this nigga definitely used a dick pump. The liquid quickly began to seep from her slightly parting lips. Quickly, her head went down onto him, letting a majority of the liquor pour free before she swiftly sucked it back into her mouth, catching every drop of the alcohol, along with vacuuming the length of him into her orifice.

"Damn..." he moaned, biting down on his bottom lip, trying to keep the whip steady as they pulled away. Her mouth was tugging the shit out of the skin on his dick, like she wanted to detach it from him.

A few minutes later, her face reappeared, lips moistened as ever as they spread into a smile.

After a breath, she hit the weed a couple of times then passed it back to him, wasting no time in getting back to the task at hand.

Shawty... damn, might fuck around and be wifey, he joked to himself, knowing good gawd damn well he wasn't about to wife no bitch. Though he had to admit that she was not bullshitting around. Watching the back of her cranium bob up and down, feeling her warm, tight mouth, he jerked to the conclusion that he'd, for sure, be the object of more tricks. "Fuck..." he grumbled between his teeth.

With one last suck and a twisting popping sound, she pulled her face from his lap again. Using both her index finger and thumb, she removed the residue of saliva from the edges of her mouth — very ladylike. "We'll save some for later, Daddy," she teased seductively with a wink of an eye.

This only geeked Q up a little more. "You must be a mind reader too? I swear I was just thinking the same thang. You already liked to made me wreck." He laughed, stuffing his shiny manhood back down into his Robins. Giving her what was left of the piff, they turned into the Waffle House parking lot. He uttered something which seemed to be a decree. "Venom, you gone fuck round and be a nigga death for real."

Only if he knew how true his words would be.

. . .

Reynolds Town sat right around the way from the hood, so it took no time for them to reach Tone's place. They parked in front of a house enclosed by a barely stable picket fence that wouldn't be able to prevent a small puppy with broken legs from escaping it. A truck sat on flat tires under a dingy car cover. Next to it was a tireless, dented up Cutlass with a missing hood and windshield. There existed not a strand of grass in the enclosure, only a few patches where weeds sprouted from the crevices of the walkway.

This nigga can't be getting no major gwop, Ace thought, letting his eyes stray over every aspect of the property. He now wanted to know the real reason as to why Whiteboy wasted his time linking up with this bum ass nigga, Tone.

I hope he ain't got my bra on no petty shit, he said to himself as they hopped out. Ace's left eyebrow lifted after he noticed that the gutter, which barely held on to the roof, appeared as if it would come down at any given moment. Then, there were wood panels missing from the front of the home, like they had taken turns falling off in certain spots, specifically around what seemed to be a living room window where the glass had been replaced by a black trash bag.

"Man, I know you ain't brought me to no crack house. " Ace chuckled yet was really serious. He instantly came to the conclusion that if Tone was in fact on some small time jugg shit, he would dead their partnership right here and now. Then, he'd give Tone the usual treatment — words equating to a chump off that were quickly followed up with a kick in the ass.

Stepping onto the porch, Whiteboy knocked on the door twice. Ace continued to inspect the scenery, wondering how many jays actually called this muthafucka home. There were enough liquor bottles and jay paraphernalia to damn near fill a junkyard. This place, he finally concluded, was a local hangout for the cracked out and clueless.

"Yeaaahhh…" They both heard someone scream out from the inside.

"This White, nigga!" Whiteboy returned loudly and a little grumpily.

"Oh, shhh…" The door quickly unlocked, then it opened. "What up, my…" Tone's voice trailed off, and his tone quickly shifted from one of excitement to a dull whisper. Tone's eyes were set on Ace. It was nothing for him to remember the 'conflict of interest' between the two of them. And likewise, he more than understood that Whiteboy and Ace were boys. Whiteboy had previously given him the ups on their relationship when they first met. But what he hadn't told him was that Ace would be accompanying them tonight. The last time Whiteboy made mention of Ace, he said Ace had been on some grieving shit and wouldn't be around for a minute. Which was why Tone neglected to fill him in on the mishaps that existed between them.

Though he — on his part — wanted no drama with Ace. Being a little more precise about it, he actually admired and respected Ace's gangsta to the fullest. He came into the game as an amateur — novice — from what Tone had heard. Then, Black, who he personally despised, groomed him, taking possession of his young mind and trans-forming him into one of the most ruthless young niggas the hood had ever produced.

Tone couldn't understand why Ace disliked him so much though. They'd never indulged in one single personal altercation. Never had a real reason to beef. Yet he felt — knew — that abhorrence was the by-product of the ill seeds planted by no other than his former comman-der, Black.

Their beef had been before Ace even thought about entering the picture. Before Tone denounced *Black Hand*.

Ace stared him up and down, realizing that Tone's appearance had done a three sixty since the last time he'd seen him. His clothes were more of the present trend — True Religion jeans, American Eagle t-shirt, Polo slippers. Then there was the Rolex wrapped around his wrist. Now that, Ace figured, most likely had been taken, probably from some white dude downtown or in Buckhead. His pockets couldn't be that deep in a shack like this.

"Ace…" Tone finally mouthed with a nod of the head, trying to avoid, beforehand, the inevitable diss in front of Whiteboy. He didn't even try to dap him up.

"Tone…" Ace returned flatly, following Whiteboy in.

"Damn, nigga. The fuck you been doing in here?" Whiteboy chuckled, cupping his nose with his hand. The strong scent seemed to be a mixture of ass, musk, weed, and liquor. All sour.

Tone fake laughed. "Man, shawty, you know a nigga was just getting in some playtime before the move. Never know when it a be ya last."

He probably was gutting out some bum ass bitch. Ace smirked, wondering who the lucky junkie had been to fall within Tone's grasp.

Whiteboy arched an eyebrow, wanting to know when he would start doing useful shit with his time, like scoping out better licks. However, he wasn't surprised. This was the norm for him since they first linked up. Tone always tried to explain his reason for such, saying, "At least if shit go wrong and I end up on the wrong side of the gun, I'd die satisfied that I busted one last nut before I left."

Of course Whiteboy couldn't blame him but damn. Everybody knew the risk of not returning before going on a lick. That was why you went harder than anybody else. What better way to guarantee a safe return?

As Tone headed down the short hallway, Ace glanced around the nastiest living room he'd ever laid eyes on. Thank God his room was in a better condition — a more livable condition than this dump. He shook his head, peering at a few labels on bottles that were scattered about the kitchen and coffee tables. There were two ashtrays over-crowded with cigarettes butts and weed roaches. The carpet needed to be shampooed badly. The vast amount of stains upon it had changed its entire texture. Then there sat the couch, which appeared to be the cleanest thing throughout the entire living area — if you didn't mind knocking away bones and crumbs of all sorts of shit. All of which could easily merge into the fabric.

"Yeah, nigga, you brought me into a fucking crack house," Ace said to Whiteboy in a tone where only they heard it.

A minute later, Tone came back into the room, spraying some cheap ass air freshener which you'd only be able to cop at a dollar store. Then, he quickly snatched a piece of clothing off the floor and began clearing places on the couch for them to take a seat.

The mist of the spray did nothing but add to the nauseating atmosphere, causing it to become even more irritating for Ace and Whiteboy.

"Man, put that shit down. You bout to kill us, nigga," exclaimed Whiteboy, pulling his shirt over his nose as he fanned the air.

Ace was forced to do the same. Tone had sprayed so much that the living room began to fog.

"Nigga, you got to have some dead pussy in this bitch," joked Whiteboy, getting a laugh from Ace.

"Man, go head on wit all that…" Tone chuckled, taking a sip of the Ice House beer he'd picked up off the table. "So, what the move is? Shawty hooked that nigga yet?" he asked, grabbing a chair.

"Yeah. She said they gone grab a bite first then…" Whiteboy let his words trail off purposely. They both knew what the plan was next.

"Oh, yeah?" he responded, partially surprised, or he pretended to be. It wasn't hard to see that he was still trying to avoid Ace's gaze at all costs.

"Yeah," Whiteboy returned, becoming a little annoyed. "I'ma GPS her phone in like another hour. Then, we gone make it do what it do."

"The nigga probably gone try to be smart and grab a hotel. So, we got to snatch 'em and apply some pressure to get the shit, you dig?" Tone finished with another sip. A longer one.

Finally, Ace felt the impulse to say something to him. "You know who dude is?" Whiteboy had already told him the part about Ariel entertaining the person they were about to move on but not to the extent of placing a name on the individual.

Tone went silent a moment, quickly sweeping his gaze between them both. "Yeah." Then, his eyes kept their place on Ace. "He used to be round the way."

Round the way wasn't hard for Ace to figure out. He understood the grimy nature of niggas in the hood. They'd set up each other at any given moment, just to put a lil something in their stomachs. But this wasn't the only hood that did it. Hell nawl. Every hood possessed this characteristic of the game.

In these streets, beneath all the glamour and hype, laid the

inevitable happenings of the malicious mind states of street niggas —
mind states which were mainly the reasons for the loss of lives in and
out of the hood. And who could blame such mind states when they
were the sole products of hunger? If you couldn't stand within the
midst of these predicaments then it would be best for you to take heed
to 2Pac's words. "If niggas can't stand the heat, then stay the fuck out
the kitchen."

"Do I know 'em?" Ace asked, feeling that more than likely he did,
which he cared less about.

"Nah. Ion think so. But you might doe. Holme used to trap at the
top of Hutchinson…" Tone said, wondering if it really mattered if he
did. Surely Whiteboy would have to be the one to keep Ace in line if
he felt some type of way in regard to their soon to be victim.

"What's his name?" Ace wasn't good at remembering names, especially when it came to those of the hood. He hadn't been the interact-
ing, social type unless it was with members of Black Hand.

"Q…" he replied, watching for any signs of recognition or anything
which would force him to become cautious.

Ace guessed he didn't want the bitch in the back to hear the name
by the way he leaned forward a little bit to say it. It was exactly how
people did when there existed a chance of other's ears catching wind of
something not concerning them.

To Ace, his reason for such was easy to comprehend but not his
logic behind the entire occasion. Why would you invite niggas over to
discuss sensitive business with a third party in the vicinity, who you
had to be wary of hearing the wrong things? That was more than just
ass backwards and all out stupid.

"Q… Q…" Ace ran the name through his mind a few times, feeling
that he might have heard it somewhere before, yet he wasn't sure. And
after a few more moments of pondering, he gave up. However, he
desperately wanted it to be a nigga he fucked with or could find a
reason to pronounce such —_anything that would give him a motive for
sending a bullet into Tone's skull. Old ways died hard.

"He racked up?" Ace now asked. Something else about this entire situation was bothering him —_rather causing him to search for a bull-shit reason to do what he should have done years ago.

"Shid, his name ringing. And I'm not talking bout amongst regular circles either."

"Nigga, that don't mean shit," Ace cut him off. "A million niggas' name ring, but that don't mean they all caked up." Ace wanted to know his incentive for targeting dude. It might establish precisely what range of digits their take would be in.

Whiteboy shook his head. He told Ace about that shit before they got here, and now he was anticipating the wrong thing falling from his lips.

"The nigga pushing a BMW XM AWD." Tone said it as if that would end all speculation.

"Tone…" Ace glared at him menacingly, leaning forward with his elbows on his knees. "Nigga, what the fuck do he got?" He wanted the full drop on him, like personal information which real robbers needed if they intended on pulling off a lucrative lick. Who the fuck moved on account of a few highlights? A various amount of dudes in the city were known for putting on with really nothing in the bank besides a few hundreds. That was the game — fake it to you make it. So, naturally, Ace felt he had no other choice but to interrogate beyond his basics. The fuck he looked like striking at thin air? Pointless.

Whiteboy glanced over at Ace. "We bout to find out, so nigga, chill…"

Ace swept his retinas between both of them, reluctantly deciding to let it go for the time being. If it turned out to be a bunch of coins in a wishing well, Ace would curse Whiteboy out for being duped into small mindedness then burn Tone for the dummy mission and because he'd introduced White and Ariel to the petty life. Lastly, he would give Whiteboy a full presentation as to how real niggas busted real moves. Not just anything. He smiled. He was back.

"Baby girl, you got a nigga begging to see what that pussy

hitting like. Shiiit!" Q growled, his head tilting backwards against the loveseat.

"Let me run this show," Ariel demanded, slowly sucking and stroking his salivated penis. She had to buy a little more time until Whiteboy and Tone showed up. At this very moment, that seemed to be taking forever. Her GPS had been activated on her phone. She'd done that at Waffle House, and after, she insisted on a hotel room of her choice. But he refused, further playing himself by making the choice of driving her to his main spot. She hadn't expected this yet was grateful that the sample of her head game brought her to such a place. Niggas were capable of doing the stupid things when their dicks did the thinking after tasting a little piece of Heaven. And being blunt about it, her mouth was a man's paradise, something that made men want to play Adam to her Eve, a female steering them toward their unfortunate demise.

They need to hurry, she thought, continuing the same routine she'd been executing for the past twenty some minutes. Q kept asking for a chance to visit that sultry, soft spot located between her legs, and she kept denying him. Yeah, she cared less about sucking a dude's dick to sleep, but Ariel wholeheartedly refused to gift out her *precious* to a random nigga, only to have him pound away at it as if it were a punching bag. No. It was specifically reserved for love.

She popped the head of his manhood out of her mouth, staring at it unbelievingly. *How could any man consider this thing to be a dick?* She smirked then wondered how badly the little guy wanted to penetrate her love. Hell, it caused Q to ask damn near every five minutes now. A few minutes went past before he'd grown bored and said, "Man, stop playing. Let's get to it for real for real."

It didn't take much for her to sense that the liquor had started to affect him. The tone of his voice had surfed a pinch of aggression her way.

Gesturing with his hand, Q stopped her from the drool session.

"Damn, bae, let me set the stage for the grand finale. I promise it a be more than worth it," she uttered sensually, pretending to be slightly tipsy as well.

"What?" he snorted. "Fuck all dat. A nigga tryna see what that pussy feel like. What? I gotta pay for it?" Q asked, coming to his feet. He let his pants fall to the floor after removing a stack of bills from them. "Here…" He broke the rubber band from the money then sprinkled some bills on her like he was sprinkling seasoning over food. Then, he laughed at her expression, stepped out of the jeans, and moved for the kitchen.

The fuck! Ariel felt disrespected yet only partially. Soon, he'd be crying for forgiveness for that little stunt. Motionless, she sat there, seeming a bit stunned by his actions. Her acid response had to be in check. She couldn't afford to mess up, especially after all the work she'd put in. Her gaze shot to him as he returned, still chuckling, a little too amused by the deed.

Q stopped in front of her with his erect penis. Staring down at her, he lifted the bottle of Moscato he'd retrieved to his lips. Right before taking a gulp, he raised an eyebrow.

"Damn, bitch, you still ain't took that shit off?" He chuckled and proceeded to drink.

"Really? You just killed the mood wit that lame ass shit." She stood, hoping Whiteboy and Tone were close — close enough to run down on him as they stepped out. "You can take me back where you found me." She was about to grab her purse until Q snatched her forcefully around.

"All them muthafucking drinks and shit a nigga done bought. Bitch, you got me fucked all the way up," he slurred, spit following behind most of his pronunciation.

"Nigga, you got the wrong bi…" Before she finished, he punched her with such power that she dropped instantly. *Shit*! Her jaw felt like it was on the verge of shattering —_if not broken already.

"Bitch, you finna take this dick…" he barked, falling on top of her. Throwing the bottle across the room, he began snatching at the leggings she wore.

"*Nooo!*" Ariel screamed, swinging at his face wildly, needing — hoping —_to make contact with something vital.

He only laughed threateningly, throwing another fierce blow then another, knocking all of the fight out of her, leaving her barely conscious.

No, not again... Not like this. She desperately wanted to gather enough strength to at least break free of him, enough to make it to the pistol in her purse. The punches he'd laid had too much effect on her body and mental. She felt like she could barely move. Ripping the fine material away from her waist, he tugged the fabric down to her knees then snatched the pink thong away from her as if it was only a mere piece of thread. She laid there, body beginning to numb. Begging to be saved by Whiteboy. Begging for something that seemed more frivolous with each passing second.

He smiled crazily, about to take what she had protected for so many years from so many like him.

"That shit smell good..." he exclaimed excitedly, shoving two fingers into her warm, wet cleavage, causing her to let out a hurtful moan. "That's right, baby. I know you ready for a real nigga."

Snatching his fingers out of her, he put them into his mouth, savoring the taste she'd been holding back. Loving the sample, Q forced her legs upward, spreading them the length the leggings would allow.

A tear treaded down Ariel's face. It was not because of the damage he intended on causing but because she was about to get raped *again!!!*

Q rubbed his manhood up and down the lips of her vagina, teasing her.

Boom! Boom! Boom!

Three hard knocks at the door echoed throughout the townhouse, interrupting the session about to take place.

Who the fuck? Q became angered by whoever it was. Bad timing. And he —_or they, he determined —_would be more than ready to get the fuck on when he was done with them.

"Patience, beautiful." He smirked, licking the side of her face. "Daddy will be right back." He got up but stopped midway, thinking to himself that people just didn't pop up at his spot by chance. No. Everyone who he allowed knew to call first and wait until he gave the okay for them to come. These visitors, he now thought, were more likely here because of his visitor.

Oldest trick in the book. Q smiled, ready to dead them and this trifling bitch. But them before her. He still had a nut to catch. Instantly, he spun around. *Damn.* He now realized his intentions would amount to nothing more than what they were. Ariel sat there with her back against the couch, aiming an almost invisible pistol at him.

After a breath, he smiled lightly, shaking his head in disbelief. "So, this what it was from the jump?" He didn't want to come to grips with reality, but he'd been caught down bad.

"And nigga, you made it more than what it was. Now open the fucking door," she hissed. Her finger was itching to slump him where he stood. However, the business wasn't finished, and plus, she wanted to make him suffer more than a bullet ever would for his transgression.

"Bitch, you real…"

Boom! The gunshot rang out loudly. She hit him in the leg and watched him stagger backwards into the wall, using it as leverage.

"Stupid bitch…" he barked in pain, grabbing at the wound with his free hand.

The door was pounded violently two more times before it caved in under the third kick.

To her surprise, Ace came through the threshold. He'd been the last person on Earth she expected to see.

His eyes landed on her immediately. He could tell by her expression what was going through her mind, yet that wasn't the only thing. Ace's gaze shifted from her to the naked man who stared at him madly. He smiled, wondering had he previously felt the way he was now.

Quickly, Whiteboy and Tone brushed past him, seeing exactly what he saw. It wasn't hard to put two and two together. The ripped clothes and their expressions spoke for itself.

Becoming enraged, Ace's next steps were toward the man.

"Don't…" Ariel said, causing him to stop short of his target. "I got other plans for that bitch."

Ace glared at him, wanting to inflict pain he never thought was possible. He wanted to make him feel the worst shit ever. Though he had to respect her wishes.

"Man, y'all nigga…" Q began but was cut off by a swift kick where he bled from. "Aghh…" Q almost fell.

"Shut the fuck up, pussy ass nigga," Ace growled, grabbing his good leg by the ankle, causing him to land flat on his back. Q attempted to kick him, which made Ace stomp his nuts then step down on his other leg until he broke his ankle.

"Aghhh, shit!" Q spit out as Ace threw his leg down.

"Now, where that shit at?"

Ace felt every bit of his old self returning quickly. He could feel that monster begging to be released from its long confinement.

Whiteboy and Tone snatched Q up by his arms and threw him over to the loveseat.

"Nigga, we ain't got all night. So, either you let us gone and grab this shit and we peel or we dead you now and tear this bitch up. You choose?" Whiteboy told him, placing the marker of his pistol on the bridge of Q's nose.

Helping Ariel up, Ace glanced at her torn clothing. "Damn, A, you good?"

"Yeah, I'm just glad to see you." She offered a slight smile. Regardless of the circumstances, she loved the fact that he was here. The streets needed him back, and he needed to reclaim them.

After a moment, Ariel dropped her gaze, trying to somewhat cover herself with what was still intact.

Ace lifted her chin then viewed each side of her face. The right side of her face was swollen, a little too swollen. "Man," he softly uttered, ready to make dude feel ten times the pain he'd made Ariel suffer. To him, any man that put their hands on women were cowards and deserved to be put in the ground. Men fought men, and women fought women. It was that simple. So, if a dude crossed the line, then someone had the right to cross his line. But then again, if a ho crossed that line, then she would also have to be dealt with in the manner necessary.

"I'm good," Ariel responded, moving her head away from his grasp.

Ace smirked, aware that she wasn't the type to be babied. She needed no special attention or caring. She always held her own like a rare type of bitch would.

Glaring, she looked over at Q as if she was ready to tear the skin from his flesh. He had tried her to the highest extent, violating her in every way, driving her to the point of not even wanting to allow him the satisfaction of thinking he'd have a chance of witnessing another day.

Ariel wanted him to understand death was inevitable. She wanted him to become more miserable with each passing second death's jaws tightened around his neck.

"Nigga, you playing," Whiteboy said through clenched teeth.

Q stared into the terrorizing face hovering over him. He could tell by the expression that he'd be dead in a few, regardless of if he told them where everything laid or not. Pitiful. He'd got caught with his drawers down. He'd gotten drunk and ran into a treacherous piece of action. He'd brought her to his spot and attempted to take what he desired. All of which left him sober and in a real fucked up position with her and her people. Q knew there existed nothing he could say that would save his life. So, he accepted his fate at this present moment and became comfortable knowing they weren't going to touch one cent of his wealth.

He smirked, ready for karma to run its course. "Nigga, you go find it," Q spit out madly.

Ace could see that dude was aware of how the situation would play out. And he saw no reason in asking again. Holme was a vet in the game and had probably gotten robbed more than a few times and likewise understood the difference in the circumstances between then and now. At this point in time, he was witnessing a whole different breed of niggas from the ones he'd played with by tossing them a little something to get them out of his face. One thing about vets in this game was that they saw the line between the pretenders and for real. They could feel it. The presence of a threat, a real one. And these three — well, four — were more than a real threat.

"Man, fuck all the playing," Ace snapped, stepping over to Q.

"Y'all tear this bitch up. He done wit." Quickly, he cocked back and swung at Q, who weaved out of the way, throwing a wild, upper swing, connecting only with Ace's shoulder.

Whiteboy gripped his wounded leg and yanked him from the loveseat. Q groaned loudly, continuing to throw all the punches he could upward, which he knew wouldn't do much. But he had to do something. Only a coward went out without a fight.

"Fuck nig…" Ace snarled, dodging swing after swing. He then pulled his strap and fell forward into the wind of blows, smashing him in the face with the pistol.

Q's head snapped to the right from the steel, causing him to cling onto Ace in an attempt to prevent the next painful hits that were bound to ensue. Whiteboy and Tone tried to pry Ace loose, while Ariel sent a fierce kick into his scrotum, forcing a cry of pain from his lips.

Almost instantly, Ace began striking him repeatedly, bringing forth spews of blood. Letting the monster take full control, Ace bashed and bashed mercilessly to the point of feeling his fingers beginning to numb from the beating.

Sixteen blows later, Q laid there battered and bloodied, slipping in and out of consciousness as they tied his wrists along with his ankles. "Go hit the rooms. We got this," said Ace, referring to him and Ariel, who was anticipating doing the most gruesome shit she'd ever thought of.

Ace peered up at her, and she understood. Without hesitation, she went into the kitchen. He smiled, wondering in which way was she about to go overboard. There was no telling. *Bride of fucking Chuckie.* Ace wanted to laugh at the inside joke, but then she came back into view with a big ass butcher's knife.

Ariel said nothing, her focus locked in on her prey. Standing within the midst of his eyes, she glared at him, allowing him a moment to take it all in.

Q's crimson colored head began to shake. His body trembled then rocked from side to side as if he wanted to wake himself from a bad dream. Yet this wasn't a dream. This was his reality with no last minute escape.

Squatting beside him, Ariel let the blade trail the length of his torso until reaching the pelvic area. She smiled gladly, gripping his penis. Digging her nails into it, she caused Q to emit a deep groan.

"Nigga, I'm about to show you another trick." She placed the knife at the root of his manhood. Ariel wanted it to become hard, so it would be easier to cut. But it remained limp like it knew what she intended.

Tugging it upward, she smiled menacingly and wasted no time in separating the sole reason for the harsh reality he was about to suffer.

Q growled in agony, making Ace grab the jeans he'd worn and stuff them in his mouth.

Ariel's smile broadened at the sight of severed flesh and blood which squirted out of him like a fountain.

His head shivered; his eyelids closed tightly. He tried to put his mind anywhere else but here. Deep moans vibrated into the denim material.

Ace knew if he hadn't been holding the jeans in place, Q's screams would be that of a deranged madman, something Ace didn't want to happen. The last thing they needed right now was for someone to hear this torment.

The puddle of his life began to form underneath him. Ariel rose to her feet, satisfied at the completed castration. She glanced downward amusingly, watching Q's body convulse. A final act was still at bay. She displayed his pride and joy before his very eyes, like that of an entrée, bearing an exotic meal. And indeed it would be.

"Ace… Get the broom," she ordered, taking a seat on his chest.

Ace swept his eyes between her and Q, really not wanting to move his hand. Q was probably waiting on a chance to yell to the top of his lungs. The muffled sounds he already exuded made that very clear.

"He can scream," Ariel told him. "That a make it even easier."

Ace removed the jeans, letting Q cough and whimper in pain. He stared at Venom with his dick in her hand, smiling gleefully. "You bitc… bitch…" he huffed wretchedly between sobs. Yes, he'd expected the worst shit. But this?

Maneuvering forward on her knees, she positioned herself over his shoulders, tightly clamping down on his neck.

Q gagged, mouth open wide as her nails dug into skin. They hurt, but now, he realized what she intended on doing. Quickly shutting his mouth, he held his lips tightly together while she guided the penis toward them. He maintained as long as he possibly could. And she bore down harder on his Adam's apple.

The severed dick was now at his lips, causing him to jerk his head away. Her nails dug farther, bringing forth blood. It was like juice from a squeezed orange.

"You bout to take this dick," Ace insisted, letting the broom fall to the carpet. Using both hands, he straightened Q's head then dug his thumbs into his eyes.

"Aghh!!!" Q yelped. His head began to quiver violently as Ace dug deeper into the sockets.

Seeing the perfect opportunity, Ariel quickly shoved the penis into his mouth, which deadened the cry immediately. His body shook where it was allowed to, that being only his lower half.

The horrific gagging started as he began to choke on himself. Out of all the ways he thought about dying, this definitely hadn't been one of them. Choking on his own dick.

Ariel leaned over, covering his mouth to keep the penis inside, and fetched the broom. She then flipped it upside down then stuck the handle in, right behind the dick. Using her weight, she thrusted both farther into his esophagus.

Q's body convulsed harder, eyes rolling to the back of his head. It seemed as though he was in the middle of a seizure. None of that mattered to Ariel; it only made it more enjoyable. She lifted, applying more pressure on the broom, shoving it downward a little farther. A terrifying gargling sound vibrated from the confines of his throat.

"Shit." Ace released his head, not worried about it moving from the position it was in. His jaw would break, and skin would shred before that happened. He looked on, astounded at how zoned out Ariel became. Her eyes were locked in place, her expression a contortion of demonical exultation. Only God knew what her mental state was at this very moment.

"Love it, nigga," she snarled lowly, repeating it as if it was a mantra, twisting the broom back-and-forth, trying to force it a bit deeper. Her action resembled that of a construction worker having a difficult time snubbing a screw in place.

A mixture of saliva, blood, and the contents he consumed this evening spewed out the corners of his mouth. The spasms of his body had calmed into a shiver. Death was now taking over. All his sounds of agony vanished, leaving his mooned eyes to scream.

Ariel kept twisting, even after realizing that Q had exited the building. She smiled. Just viewing his tortured facial display made her want to continue. It was marked with misery, terror, suffering, and death, and she loved every minute of it. His painful departure had been worth watching.

"Ariel…" Ace finally called out, realizing how lost in the moment she'd become. He'd just watched her take every piece of the man's pride and life. Even though he was clearly gone, she continued to suffocate his corpse. And Ace knew why. He was very aware of her past, which motivated her present state of mind. Who could fault her?

Finally, her hands released the broom, and she looked up at Ace. The broom had forced Q's head to turn sideways, as it hit the floor, though still lodged into his throat. Nothing came from her mouth in return. Her eyes only locked with his before he took her into his arms. He whispered, "You good, Ma? You did what you had to."

It had been a minute since he'd actually seen her — held her. But nevertheless, her beauty remained intact besides the bruises she'd acquired tonight.

He stared at her, wondering how she'd managed to keep herself up after all this time. After all the things she'd been through. Whatever it was, she had quite obviously perfected it.

Ace found it hard to avert his eyes away from her. Thoughts of the first time he laid eyes on her came flooding back to his mind. It was a time when things were in place and were good.

When they'd first met, Ace thought she was one of the *typicals* in search of a nigga to leech on to, something he loathed. But to his surprise, she was nothing like any female he'd encountered before. She displayed a set of impeccable standards, which she refused to alter on account of any nigga. And that was what hooked him. Ariel possessed real morals, along with a killer instinct, which no female he'd met could lay claim to. Then, her hustle game and mouthpiece were on point.

It had amused him so much that he didn't bother to ask. So, he demanded that she join his team. And she didn't bother to think about it. To Ariel, his demeanor said all that she needed to know. He had boldly told her that she would be by his side, and she was impressed. This had been a first, and she liked it.

The way he handled the situation and her, she couldn't help but to admit that he made her feel as though she needed his domination. His masculine control made her pussy wet, to the point of exploding between her legs every time he ordered something done without the slightest input from her.

To her, he was the representation of a natural born leader. A king amongst men. A rarity, which was why she allowed him to practically run over her. She knew, though, that it would only be a matter of time before he'd realize the type of female he'd recruited and the qualities that came along with her. However, there existed a deeper craving within her. She wanted him in more ways than just a mere partnership. Ace's persona spoke every characteristic of the man she longed for. Of course she was aware of his female companion before he even mentioned it. Shoot, what female in their right mind would let a guy of his caliber pass by without clinging on to him? So, she was unfazed by that part.

Everything from the depths of her soul to the surface of her skin told her she had to have a taste. A piece of a moment with him. He perfectly fit the description of guys in urban novels —_not perfect yet lustful in so many ways. How many times had her heart ached to feel him? She seduced him. Many nights she dreamed of everything he had to offer. She kissed him. Too many words she thought of to encourage him to take all of her. She fucked him.

Nothing could be compared to the way they sexed each other. It was that of two wild animals biting, scratching, and tousling over one another until their bodies collapsed from explosive climaxes.

Ace continued to stare into the depths of her eyes, his mouth inching closer to hers. It had been a while since the last time he stood so close to intimation. He felt as if he should hold back, but something deep within pronounced that it was right. Or at least made him feel as though. Sassy had died. And she couldn't be replaced, period. So he became content with remaining lonesome. Hell, he felt nothing since her death. Well, until now.

He couldn't understand his feelings. Maybe it was due to all of those months he went without the presence of a female, or it might have been Ariel's aura. He hadn't felt that burning sensation earlier when he bumped into Michelle. She only possessed a few qualities to cause a hard on.

This feeling he now experienced was a little more than mere lust. But it wasn't that of what he had and lost. His lips were right at the edge of hers. He could almost taste her breath.

"Say…" Ace heard Whiteboy's voice from behind them. Quickly, he receded to face him. Evidently, he'd caught them in the act. The stupid smirk on his face said it all. Ariel smiled shyly. She knew Whiteboy was silly as hell and would definitely make a few jokes about it later on.

"What?" Ace finally asked, a bit irritated by the way he just stood there, staring at them, smiling.

"We found a little something. Come to the back room when you two siblings finish the lil cute reunion." He laughed, turning to head back, but stopped. "And by the way, how y'all muthafuckas gone do all that over that?" he questioned, pointing at the lifeless body of Q. "But I'm the crazy one. Please."

Ace and Ariel laughed, embarrassed, as they followed behind him.

BACK IN THEIR APARTMENT, ACE SAT AT THE TABLE, SIPPING ON AN orange juice as he listened to Ariel tell him things he'd previously heard from Whiteboy. Yet and still, he listened, though more because of the way she recounted the events. She was so pretty. The way she smiled and talked with that beautiful laugh — here and there —_had him ready to hear her entire life story over again. The way she moved, whipping her shoulder length hair from her face, caused him to become transfixed. Her teeth were in perfect line with one another, sparkling every time she parted her lips. Her tongue flicked sexually with each pronunciation. Eyes were magnetic, drawing him into her realm of conflagration, igniting his soul. Compelling his manhood to burn with anticipation.

Ace stared, hypnotized, unable to tear his gaze away from the one thing he desired to caress, tame, and sex dangerously.

As she continued, he began to think about the last time he'd laid with her and how she'd drained and exhausted him. It had been intense, pleasurable, passionately painful, and… innovative. His dick jumped at the thought, begging him to execute whatever it took to cruise her highway of femininity. He guessed she felt the harmonic vibrations from his shaft because her eyes began to speak an orgasmic dialect.

Their eyes met.

Ariel missed the way his dick penetrated every part of her sultry Heaven, the way it created energetic friction inside of her, shooting an implosive, breathtaking charge throughout her entirety.

Their gazes locked, enveloped in an intoxicating exchange, while the pheromones of their bodies mingled in a dance of desire.

Taking her hand, Ace lifted it to his mouth and began kissing the palm softly. A mellifluous moan escaped her mouth. Their eyes locked in an unspoken connection as he delicately slid her middle finger into his mouth. Her body responded. This made her hot to the point that she could feel the primal heat between her legs intensify, forcing the tantalizing moistness of her own juices to soak into the silky fabric of her panties. Her body tensed. She bit down on her bottom lip, watching him seductively lick his way to each finger, initiating the same routine as he'd done to the first one. Finished, he licked his lips and grinned. He was ready to use all of the fluids of his mouth on another part of her. And as well, she was more than ready for him to place his soft lips on her concealed ones.

Ariel's subconscious encouraged her to rip off everything she had on, yet her womanhood demanded that she make him work for it in the roughest way. The scenery encircling them faded away, leaving nothing but their animalistic nature to tango.

Every part of this moment seemed perfect; well, that was until Whiteboy interrupted. "Man, y'all two…" he said, shaking his head.

In unison, they both gave expressions which said only one word. *Bye!*

Obviously, he'd caught their drift. "Aight, I'm finna dip. But man, keep all that shit out of my room." He smirked, snatching the rental keys from the table.

"Don't be early." Ace smiled, giving him a wink of the eye.

"Shid, you don't be, nigga," Whiteboy quickly shot back, pulling the door open.

Quickly, Ace stepped over to it, making sure it had locked behind him. The last thing he needed was for him to return in the middle of their session unexpectedly. And now that he thought about it, he wished he would have subtracted the apartment's keys from the key ring. That could have ensured it. Pivoting back around, he was face-to-face with Ariel. Her eyes trailed over his physique lustfully. It was as if she couldn't wait another second to sink her teeth into him.

Being the only thing he could think of, he pulled her close, brushing his nose against the edge of hers. Instantly, he became aroused by that succulent aroma her body exuded heavily. Starting at the side of her face, he placed small, soft kisses across her forehead. Her tongue slid over the skin of his neck, slowly inching its way downward to the rhythm of his movement.

Her hands roamed underneath his t-shirt, gliding across the rippling surface of his abs, exploring every inch of every crease they possessed. Nothing excited the spot between her legs more than an exotically toned man.

Ace took his t-shirt completely off and gripped her waist, letting his tongue find the dwelling of her mouth. Their kiss was passionate, igniting both of their souls.

Feeling more than ready, Ariel jitterily undid his belt and pants. And as she was about to pull them down, he stopped her. Giving her a peck on the lips and chin, Ace turned, leading her toward the kitchen table. He positioned her facing it. Standing behind her, he slightly pushed her forward, causing her to use the table for balance.

An almost inaudible moan escaped her lips as he grinded the bulge of his jeans against her apple bottom ass. His tongue slid along the nape of her neck. He loved the way her skin tasted.

Rhythmically, her buttocks swayed from side to side, accompanying his motion. His hands went down into the sweatpants she wore. Damn, he wanted to say. Her body was radiating heat through its coat of velvety. forcing his manhood to stiffen appropriately for the burglary of paradise. Gripping the line of her panties, he forced them down, along with the sweats slowly. Ace wanted to enjoy every revealed piece of flesh inch by inch. He admired the perfect shape of her ass, and even more so, he loved the smell it gave off. It was a smell which could live in his nostrils forever.

Finally, he let the material settle at her ankles. He went to his knees. Ace's gaze locked in on the magnificent sight, mouth salivating for a taste. But patience…

Lubricating two fingers, he positioned them between her legs, making soft contact with the edge of her love box. Slowly, he slid them from her love toward the length of her ass crack after pausing a brief moment to let the tip of his middle finger penetrate her rectum.

"Ohh…" Ariel gasped while he inched deeper into her ass, twisting as it went a little farther. He stroked the walls of her anal passionately then pulled his finger out, cleaning it with the insides of his mouth, preparing it for another trip.

"Mmm… shit," she let out. He slapped her voluptuous ass before helping her step out of the clothing which wouldn't be necessary for hours.

Legs now free, Ariel pushed backwards, spreading her legs farther apart. She smirked, wanting Ace to see all of what he'd have to take care of. Seductively and slowly, she sexually rotated her hips. She was more than ready to receive whatever he chose to offer, hopefully something a bit more than she could bear.

Parting the cheeks, his tongue instantly sprang out. His face went forward, shoving itself in between them. Her juices instantly saturated his tongue before it even entered her vagina.

"Damn…" softly escaped her lips. She eased up on her tiptoes. Her body slightly trembled from the lovely sensation which quickly shot through her. How could his strongest muscle make her feel weak so quickly? She had to ask herself.

His tongue flicked strongly against her spur tongue before launching itself as far as it could into her orifice. More of her flowed into his mouth. He swallowed, feeling all he'd missed massage into the pores of his face. *Damn, she taste so good.* He began sucking what he could out of her — hopefully all of her.

Letting a few moments pass, Ace slid his tongue the length of her ass then impatiently eased it against the outer layer of her anal. Forging a small mountain of salvia toward the edge of his tongue, he caused it to become stiff.

"*Ahh!*" she huffed as his delicate instrument penetrated. "Fuck, Ace…" She leaned forward a bit more, wanting to run — wanting him to force more into her. Ariel's eyebrows arched, and she bit farther into her bottom lip. Fuck, she loved the way it felt. Ace rhythmically wiggled inside of her, refusing to let a spot within her go without being touched. Her ass tensed and pulsated every time he twisted as much as he could into her.

Reaching, he placed his hands onto her back, pushing her forward a little more. How determined he was to taste all of her.

"Shit, boy!" she moaned louder, wishing he'd stick his whole damn head into her tight ass. She couldn't begin to explain the way she was feeling. It only felt that if he continued, surely her ass would cum on his tongue, mouth — face. All of her stomach muscles clenched together. Her legs shivered weakly from this well missed pleasure. It had been too long since the last time she'd experienced this blessing. "Fuck!!!"

Palming and spreading both cheeks apart, Ace finally came up for air. He admired the panoramic view and especially at how moist he'd made it. The sight turned him on even more, compelling him to place his face where it had been, launching every inch of his tongue back into her.

Ariel's body jerked forward, wanting to run from the pleasure of his visage. Definitely, he was trying to get it all. "A-Ac..." she stuttered as he started back excavating her ass.

Giving it one last deep dig, he came to his feet, leaving a hand to slide up and down her butt crack as though it was therapeutic. He glanced down, feeling how wet he'd left it. How hot it had gotten.

Moving his free, unoccupied hand over her stomach, he lifted her torso toward him, keeping his other one between those soft ass cushions she possessed.

Her head craned sideways. She reached behind him, gripping the back of his neck. A smile stretched across her face upon noticing that he left his tongue out for cleaning, exactly what she'd been thinking. Tugging his head toward her, she sucked it into her mouth without hesitation. Instantly, she could taste her very own fluids mix with her saliva before sliding its way down into her throat — as if this was the normal routine.

Ace loved this about her. Ariel knew when it was time to be a lady and when it was time to be a fucking animal.

Breaking the loving tangle of their mouths, Ariel pivoted around, facing him. Her hands quickly went to undoing his pants. Finishing with the zipper, she slid them down, lowering herself along with them. His erect manhood slapped against the bottom of her chin once it was free. Her eyes locked in on his shaft. She smirked, remembering how pretty it had been. and it still was now. Letting her tongue fall out, she removed the pre-cum oozing from the tip of him. Ariel was partly surprised at how ready her mouth was to please Ace's nature. It salivated to the point of damn near overflowing. Maybe it had been the sight of the veins protruding beneath the skin of his dick. Or maybe it was just him.

Pretty ass dick. She parted her lips to receive as much of him as she could accept.

A muffled growl vibrated from his throat. Her mouth felt warm and a little too soft to be real. Her lips tightened, stroking the flesh of him passionately. Saliva gushed forth every time her head bobbed back and forward. Hands free, Ariel picked up her pace, stroking him harder. A little faster. Each time twisting and turning her head roughly when she came to the tip of him.

"Shhh…" flew from his lips. He gripped the top of her cranium to slow her down some. At this rate, he knew he wouldn't last for too long.

Nonetheless, she continued sucking harder until she glanced up, catching sight of his facial expression. She wanted to burst out laughing. Ace was biting down on his knuckles with one eye closed, eyebrows extra arched. Ariel smiled, having realized now that she was inflicting some deep shit which he hadn't experienced in over a year. "Too much, huh?" she teased, ready to make him want to chew his whole damn hand off.

"Who?" he said after a deep breath. "Please." He refused to give her the pleasure of knowing she was on the verge of making him tap. That would be embarrassing, especially after all the times he'd laughed at her tapping out. She'd surely hang the shit over his head every time they fucked, something he couldn't have. Ace glanced down at his well lubricated penis. "Man, what the fuck she talking bout? Gotta show her who she fucking wit." He chuckled, slapping it against her chin playfully.

"We'll see; y'all must've forgot. It been a minute for you both." Without wasting another second, Ariel went back in. Yet this time, more ambitiously. She became determined to break his ego, especially after witnessing how she'd had him.

Specks of spit were slung to her shirt, some down her arm as she plunged him in and out of her mouth ferociously. Every few thrusts, she'd force him in until his manhood punched her tonsils, causing her to gag and spew up more saliva.

"Shit. Eat that shit," Ace grumbled, fucking her face, pausing only briefly to free his ankles from the pants. The moment was about to get too intense to be restricted in space. After allowing her to get her *stunt* on, Ace pulled backwards then bent over, kissing her directly in the mouth, slowly bringing her to her feet. Picking Ariel up by her ass, he gently placed her onto the table.

Without having to be instructed, she spread her legs wide open, giving him a beautiful shot of vagina. He had to give it a kiss and a big one at that. Lord knew he'd be wrong if he didn't.

Smuuush! The sound had loudly resonated from the twisting of the two sets of lips. Wet mouthed and smiling, he rubbed his shaft up and down the split of her lips teasingly then positioned right where he intended on penetrating. Using both thumbs, he parted her lips, guiding himself between the gates of Heaven.

"Ohh, Ace!" she exhaled, letting her retinas roll toward the ceiling, feeling her tight, succulent pussy stretch around him. Her head fell backwards as he entered her at an angle, digging into her deeper and deeper.

Damn, he wanted to say. Her pussy felt so good to him that he had to take his time, or he'd bust, disappointedly, a little bit too early. Plus he wanted to savor a minute of it. It had been way too long.

"Fuck me," Ariel now demanded. She wanted to feel every bit of his masculine thrust. And now, he would let her. Spreading her legs farther apart, he forced himself strongly within her crevice, causing her to jerk upward in an attempt to close her legs. But he refused the action. She'd begged for this.

Quickening his pace, he began to pound away at her harder, deeper, bringing more of her juices from within her. "Fuck!!!" she screamed from the pleasure, pain, and passion that was resonating throughout her entire body. *Shout out to that nigga, Trey Songz,* she wanted to yell, but the words were caught up in her throat. It felt like he was hitting the bottom of her esophagus. He was pounding all of her words into a cluster. She hadn't experienced this in a year. He was piercing every piece of her insides. Or at least that was what it felt like. Yes, his dick was hurting, doing damage, but was also healing her flesh and soul, all at the same time. And she wouldn't want it any other way unless a duplicate was here with them now, keeping her mouth occupied, wedging all of her sounds between both dicks.

Ace gripped the underside of her thigh, pushing it backwards as he dug her shit out, rotating his hips, needing to feel all of her. He had to remind her who he was and who owned this pussy. Pressing down on the lower part of her stomach with his hand, the other balanced him over the table. Steadily, he launched himself harder into her wet ocean. Splacking sounds from their collisions reverberated loudly throughout the kitchen. This only caused Ace to quicken and harden his thrusts.

"Fu-fuck, Ace!" Ariel yelled out, her eyes closed and her forehead wrinkled. Placing a foot on his hip was how she hoped to slow him down. But it was to no avail. He relentlessly hammered away at her love. Okay, it was nothing like this the last time. This felt a lot more painful. A lot better. Well, two times better.

"Damn, girl," he huffed, keeping his rhythm intact as he glanced down at the action of their organisms, wishing like hell he was his dick. He just wanted to get a real view of what was inside the pussy to make a nigga feel like this. Her vagina went a tad over being wet; juices sprang forth as though it was a Greek fountain. There had been enough to mark a territory, which was his entire genital area. This aroused him more.

Taking her foot into his hand, Ace lifted it to his mouth and succulently began kissing on the bottom of it. First, at the heel, then he slowly inched his way to her big toe. All at the same time, he kept his motion persistent, yet at little slower. More melodized. He sucked away lecherously, enjoying the way her foot tasted. Damn, it was like all of her was good for eating.

Digging harder, deeper, Ace slid his tongue from toe to toe, giving them all the attention they deserved.

"Bae, I… I… I'm… finna… *cum!!!*" she moaned sexually. As well, his orgasmic momentum was building. He knew that he was only a few thrusts away from exploding within her.

"Fuccckkk!" Her mouth opened as her nails sank into his neck, others breaking the skin on his forearm. Her body began to shake, vibrating into a few hard jerks. A thick layer of cream foamed out of her, slowly melting away into their skins.

"Shit!" Her head fell backwards, eyes witnessing what was on the inside of her skull. "Hol' up," she let out between deep breaths. Her body began to convulse. Her vagina tickled from the exotic sensation. "Please, Ace... Pu-pull that... m-muthafucka out!" she gasped pleadingly.

He eased himself to a slow stroke, wanting her to beg him to stop. Ace smiled amusingly, loving the way her heavenly milk covered his nature. Damn, this had to be the prettiest picture on Earth. Well, one of them. Surely, before the night was over, more picturesque moments would occur. He chuckled, staring down at her situation as she tried to calm herself. Definitely, he'd put her in a worst condition then she'd put him in.

"Too much, huh?" he asked mockingly, using her exact words from minutes ago. He then pretended like he was about to slide two fingers into her.

"No, no, no..." she quickly squealed, scooting backwards, knocking over a bottle and glass which were behind her.

"Stop playing." He laughed, grabbing onto her foot.

"Boy, stop. Hold on. You just made me orgasm," she said, placing a hand in front of her coochie. Of course she loved every bit of how she came. But it was way more than she'd expected. And yes, she wanted it again and again. But right now though, her vagina was a little too sensitive for him to ram that rod back into her. They'd have all night, and she was far from finished.

Passionately, he began placing small kisses onto the bottom of her foot. "We got a long night ahead of us..."

She smirked, thinking this was about to get real intense and insane. It would be a night to remember.

CHAPTER THREE

"Yo, B, I'm still trying to find out how you actually found this place," Dawg said to Trigga as they sat inside a rental car. They were in the parking lot of Amsterdam Walk.

Amsterdam Walk was a five-star plaza where only the paid, rich, and famous shopped when vacationing in Atlanta. It wasn't one of those everyday breeze *bys* for the regulars either. That was obvious. The trees which surrounded the plaza were doing their jobs perfectly by ducking the place off and out of sight from the prying eyes of unfortunates and wannabes. You couldn't just drive by. The plaza also sat down a street which would cause you to assume that nothing outside of a few houses and those damn trees that laid at the end existed.

The Walk, as some had titled it, consisted of no more than eight to nine shops and two restaurants. All were top of the line for top-of-the-line people. And yet, here sat two underprivileged individuals as patrons of the small location.

Trigga had found *The Walk* one evening when searching the internet for a wedding ring. He was intending on using a diamond out of a Van Cleef & Arpels wedding ring as a proposal gift for his aggravating ass girlfriend. Then, he came across this particular place though never had his ears caught wind of the words Amsterdam Walk, let alone a jewelry shop called 'Glorified Diamonds, which contained his gift. And after GPS'ing the place, he couldn't help but to let it grab his full attention.

It was crazy that it was situated damn near in the heart of 4th Ward, an area he swore he'd covered every inch of. But here it was, sitting beyond the sights of *unwanteds*, offering a perfect opportunity for this unwanted to take advantage of.

Robbing jewelry and electronic stores had been the nine to five which put food on his table and into the stomachs of his team. While at the same time, it ensured that he was en-route to becoming a young entrepreneuric-millionaire at the age of twenty-three. That was one of the things he more than realized would become true, especially after giving this store's merchandise a quick eye estimate. He couldn't help but to display an extra big grin.

Pure diamonds, flawlessly imbedded in watches, rings, necklaces, and bracelets filled the cases that lined both sides of Glorified Diamonds, ending in an 'U' connection at the far end of the place. Two cameras existed. One was situated at an angle over in the left corner, and the other sat farther back, directly opposite of the other. Both equated to the only security presence as far as he could tell after a few visits.

Perfect lick had been written all over it. Trigga, one visit at a time, placed a value on each of the twelve cases and figured that he'd knock over the place for nothing less than a mill. And a mill he was determined to have.

He let out a slight laugh. "Nigga, you gone think I'm bullshitting if I tell you."

"Hell, try me," returned Dawg, sweating the fat ass in the tight leggings. *The white girl is blessed to be carrying all that on her back*, Dawg thought as she made her way past the two of them.

"Shid…" Trigga began rubbing on his chin. "My nigga, I was looking for a finger piece for my ruby and fucked around and came across this hard ass, iced out piece wit the diamonds laced around the main stone and continuing around the band of that muthafucka." He fished through his phone for the picture he'd saved. After pulling it up full screen, he shoved it in front of Dawg's eyes.

"Word," Dawg huffed, understanding exactly his motive for locking in on this particular spot when they had other stuff lined up. The ring alone was an expensive piece compared to the other whatnots they had on their agenda. It had been a rare jewel he'd never seen. It was something far from what an average dude would put on somebody's finger. And likewise, he knew just like Trigga did that more iced out *tagalongs* would be found at the same place. Dawg believed in the saying, "Birds of a feather flock together."

"You ready?" asked Trigga, stashing his pistol under the seat.

"Word." Dawg imitated the movement with his own strap.

The two stepped out into the morning breeze and quickly treaded their way up the stairwell. After they strolled past a few stores, Trigga noticed, like he had done all the other times, that they also had valuable items worth taking as well, like the one they'd just went by, which advertised 'Ray Fish' footwear. He already knew the price range of the weird looking shoes was fourteen bands or more. Then, there set a watch place which sold from Rolexes to Shinolas to Breitlings, and last but not least, Cartiers.

Trigga wasn't much into the pop star clothing shit, but the clothing store that separated the watch spot and Glorified Diamonds had a few things that would be worth his attention at a later date, along with the rest of Amsterdam's prizes.

Pulling open the door to Glorified Diamonds was like opening the doors to a paradise of diamonds. The store glistened from the cases, sparkling in all directions. Trigga guessed this was what it looked like when people entered treasured tombs. Foreign paintings clutched onto the walls, along with a few pictures of up-to-date celebrities who he guessed had purchased jewelry from them. Only five employees occupied the place. As far as he could tell, three of them were busy tending to other patrons as the other two watched them as they stepped in.

"Welcome to Glorified Diamonds where diamonds are glorious," the middle aged, foreign guy spoke, giving Trigga and Dawg that fake ass salesman smile. It was evident that they were not anything close to their usual visitors.

Trigga said nothing, only gave a nod of the head as he made his way toward the Black female he intended on talking to. Hell, he'd spoken to every other employee before. And plus, she'd been the only Black employee he'd seen out of all those other times.

She smiled a little after witnessing the two newcomers ignore her supervisor, heading straight toward her.

"Welcome to Glorified Diamonds…"

Trigga cut her short from reciting the same introduction the foreigner reluctantly offered. "How you, Ma?" he softly asked, extending his hand to her.

"Great and you?" She smiled, taking his hand.

"Aight until I seen you…"

Her facial expression quickly faded from cheery to one of confusion. "Excuse me?"

He chuckled at her sudden facial expression change. "Damn, Ma, are you gone let me give you a compliment before you start frowning?" Trigga had caught her off guard with that one. He could tell by the way she began to laugh a little, a tad embarrassed.

"And that's?" she asked, wondering what type of slick stuff he was about to utter.

"Shid, I was aight. But seeing you made a nigga day a lot better, beautiful… Alethea."

She blushed some, realizing he paid at least some attention to a few details other than the ones of her physique. "Well, thank you. I'm grateful… Now, how may I help you today, Mister…" She now wanted to know the name of the cute, unusual individual.

"No, Mister. Just call me Corleone," he said seductively.

"Okay, Mr. Corleone, what would you like today?" She intended for her words to be placed a little smartly, not flirty.

"You serious?" He chuckled, eyeing her up and down.

Instantly, she got his point, thinking about how the words had sounded leaving her lips. Somehow, they'd been unintentional but in need of some quick doctoring. "Jewelry, that is…"

"I bet," Trigga said, causing her to give him another look. "Just playing, Ma. But I wanted to check out some of you all's ear shots."

"Ear what?" she questioned, lost on the slang.

He twisted his lips into a smirk. "Earrings. Tired of these." Trigga gave her a clear view of them.

Diamonds were her thing, so it didn't take long for her to realize that he'd coughed up a nice sum of money for the stones in his ear.

"Okay, step over here and we'll see what we can do about that."

Trigga followed her around to the other case, across from where Dawg and another employee were discussing something inaudible to him. They came to a stop a few inches away from where a foreign female employee stood, helping this mixed couple with what appeared to be engagement rings. He looked at Alethea, who was squatting behind the counter, pulling out a tray of earrings. *Damn, I wished I could see her squat like that at the crib.* He watched her place the tray on the case, sliding it toward him without hesitation.

Judging by the set he already had in his ears, she knew he would want the best they had to offer, which was now being positioned between the two of them.

Musing over the pieces, he thought about how he could easily pull a quick scratch and grab, skills his previous occupation required. But that would be some petty shit. Nah, he was going to take majority of all of this store's shit and not some lil stuff like most of the niggas in the city were doing nowadays.

After a moment, he decided to flex a bit, thinking he'd kill two birds with one stone.

"You choose." He insisted on having what she'd thought would be the best choice.

Her head tilted some. She was shocked by his words and lost on why he'd want someone, who knew nothing about his taste or what he'd prefer, to pick. And to top it off, she was clueless as to the type of money he was trying to let Glorified Diamonds consume. Alethea couldn't help but to stare, speechlessly wondering if he was serious. Then, she quickly got her answer as the tray slid back toward her. She placed her hand on it, causing it to cease its movement.

"Oh… Uh, how am I supposed to know which ones are for you? I don't know your budget or preference."

"Does it matter?" Trigga quickly returned, pulling two thick bundles of bills from his pockets.

Her eyes, along with the other jewelers' and the couples', locked in on the money as if it was taboo.

"Uh…Obviously not," she returned. She was kind of impressed, but a Black card would have been more impressive.

"Well, choose then." He smiled, taking a quick glance at the other spectators, who were still transfixed on the bands that he let purposely fall onto the counter.

Alethea stared at him another moment then dropped her eyes to the tray of jewels. She'd already had the prices of some of them in her head, which were mostly the costly ones. The same ones, she figured, he'd stunted for. "How about…" She started but paused as one finger floated over the earrings like this was a puzzling choice. After a few seconds, her finger landed on a pair. "How about these?" she finally said, searching his face for approval.

"Bet. Ring 'em up," Trigga uttered nonchalantly with an air of cockiness. He began to remove the rubber bands, clapping the money together like they were chalkboard erasers.

She smirked, shaking her head as she picked up the pair from the tray and placed the tray back where it had been. "Mr. Corleone, that will be… eleven thousand and four hundred dollars." Alethea carefully watched him after ringing up the total.

"Aight, don't bag 'em. I'm bout to put them in now," he told her after handing over what she'd requested while adjusting the counter's mirror. "Say, Alethea?" He started removing one of the earrings from his ear.

"Yes?"

"So, what you gone wear?"

"Wear?" she returned, not understanding.

"What are you going to wear tonight when we hit Bacchanalia?" He was now replacing the second earring.

Alethea chuckled, slightly amused at his slickness. "I don't think my boyfriend would like that."

Trigga chuckled. "Shid, I never seen a nigga get mad at something he don't know." He gave her a look like *be for real.*

"Well, he would because I'm just that faithful." She tried her best to sound confident.

"Yeah, but that's until he makes you mad, whereas you'd be searching for some pastime entertainment to relieve your mind from the moment's crisis," he assured her.

"I'm pretty sure I can manage a *crisis* all by myself, Mr. Corleone."

"I guess for now." He winked his eye, fastening the screw on the second earring.

"For now." She smiled.

"Yeah, aight." He returned a friendly smile, placing the old set of earrings into the box. "See you later, Miss Alethea." He slowly took the receipt, giving her one more overlook before heading toward the entrance.

CHAPTER FOUR

"Shawty, man, this lil bitch, RJ, be playing wit a nigga," said Spain as he and Kero leaned up against the car in the gas station parking lot. They were right across the street from Crim open campus. This had been an *every other* day routine for the two. They would post up, waiting for the school to let out the next action they'd seduce into going back to the hood with them, so they could smash. Then, they'd pass her off to the rest of the niggas at the spot, like she was a cup getting passed around a ritual ceremony. Their new rip today would make the fourth chick this week, and it was only Wednesday.

"Man, I told you that ho ain't nothing but some jump off, and you still gone try to main her. Now look at you sweating ova the bitch." Kero chuckled as he finished licking the blunt together.

"Nigga ain sweating a bitch ass thang," returned Spain brashly. "But I'm not gone flex either. Shawty a bad lil bitch, and she got some fye."

Kero gazed at him a second with a look that said, "Nigga, please." Then, he said, "I know that's right." He laughed, knowing his lil partner was drunk over shawty. It was evident. Spain constantly called her and always wanted to pull up on her whenever they had some free time to fuck around. Spain was definitely head over heels for the little freak, and even Kero had to admit that he could sort of see why. RJ was one of the baddest young hos that they'd seen at the school. But regardless of how sexy she was, no bitch — in Kero's opinion — was to be drunk over or chased. To him, females were similar to the Rubix cube. Fun to play with at first. Difficult to figure out and complete after a nigga's hard work.

Many patterns it could be manipulated into, exactly like females' mood swings, which would make it even more complicated the longer a nigga dealt with it. And that was until he finally got tired of it and tossed the damn thing to the side, which was the best part to him.

"Get the fuck outta here," chuckled Spain, giving him a light push.

Spain glanced over at the entrance of the school building, seeing that a few students were coming out, just nothing like the regulars who usually flooded out. They were early. Yet how early? he began to wonder because the two had been sitting here for a little over fifteen minutes.

Looking down at his G-Shock, the time read two-twenty. *Only ten more minutes*, he said to himself. He turned back toward Kero, who had the piff between his lips, about to fire up.

"Man, you tripping," Spain snapped a little, slapping his hand, causing the flame to go out.

"What?" Kero let out, displaying an awkward expression.

"Man, you know twelve be pulling up here when they let out."

"Nigga, so?" Kero spit back, irritated. He hated when somebody tried to come between him and his flight lessons.

"Aight, so. Ain trying to get booked witcha ass."

"Man, come on wit that jinxing ass shit." Kero snatched the blunt from his lips, hoping this lil nigga didn't talk it into existence. "You know how to fuck some'n up, lil nigga."

"I know how to keep *our* asses from getting jammed and fucked up, lil nigga," Spain returned mockingly.

Kero's head tilted backwards, letting his face lift toward the sky, knowing that he was right yet hating it. On more than one occasion,

Spain had saved both of them from the ill fate of the county jail and worst. He couldn't help but to smirk.

"My lil nigga," he whispered to himself, loving how his lil partner stayed aware of all the possibilities. Though sometimes, it irked the hell out of him by how cautious he was capable of being. "That's what up," Kero mouthed, cuffing the piff in his hand as he continued. "Let me ask you some'n, lil bra."

Spain gazed at him a moment, preparing himself to hear some kind of stupidness, which was quite regular for his mouth. "What up?"

"I talked to Ariel this morning, and she was telling me how Ace was back at it and how he ready to get the team back on the same page like it used to be…"

"Oh, yeah? That's the move. Big bra gone turn this shit back up." Spain cut him off, excited, then he quickly noticed the grim look on Kero's face. Obviously, Kero had something different on his mind. What, though, was the question. "What up, bra?"

"What up?" Kero started smartly. "Nigga, you say that shit like that's really what's up or some'n."

"Wha…" Spain huffed, surprised and caught off guard by what was coming out of Kero's mouth.

"Lil nigga, you must forgot about how he just up and left us out to dry, and you talking bout that's what up," he finished, releasing the air out of his lungs. He was blown by the mere fact that Spain could even think that shit was all good.

Clearly this nigga on some more shit, Spain thought as he stared at him. "You tripping. Nigga, this Ace you mouthing bout, fool."

"Nigga, I know. The same Ace that gave us his word that he'd never up and leave a nigga out there. The same muthafucking Ace that made all us take an oath till death do us part. And one of us leaving the rest out there was nowhere in that muthafucka."

Spain couldn't help but to smirk, as if brushing it off. He didn't want to reveal how heated on the inside Kero was making him. "Nigga, so what the fuck would you have done if his shoes were on your feet? If niggas snatched up somebody you loved, gunned both of y'all down?" He spit it out a little aggressively. Though he was trying to keep his composure, he still found it hard to believe that Kero actually felt some type of way, especially toward someone who'd done so much for all of them. Toward somebody that was the main reason they still had their space carved out into the streets.

Kero smiled. Spain's words were quite amusing. "Nigga, that's why I don't love. If a bitch catch me, they gone catch me by myself, so you know it's gone gunz up." He laughed, turning his fingers into guns, aiming them at Spain in a playful manner.

"So, if a nigga don't love, that a mean that you don't love us? How are we to expect him to stand firm on the shit we all took an oath to?" Spain asked, trying to sound as logical as possible. His words had struck a nerve, he could tell. It was written all across Kero's face, which only seconds ago was other than what it was now.

Kero bore into him coldly for a moment, letting the words of his mouth bounce around within his mental. Spain, he knew, couldn't even begin to understand how he really felt. Kero had been on Ace's side since he'd first jumped off the porch into this street life. They had eaten together, killed together, along with surviving the ill doings of Black together.

They were bonded by their circumstances. Their struggles. Their loneliness. Their ups and downs had been wielded together. So together was the only way they'd weather the storm of life.

Yet, over a period of time, a crack found its way into their cemented canvas of loyalty and trust. A seam which spread with every arrogant and cocky action Ace began to display. In his eyes, Ace gradually changed from the young, shy, terrified little boy he'd once been to the murderous and prideful, strong arm of Black, an arm that was entitled to all sorts of benefits.

This was what put the icing on the cake. Ace and Kero had put in major work. Had brought good bread to the table by their works, but Ace's plate was always loaded with more than his and others. The same irritation he felt long ago began to slowly tread back through his veins, exactly like it had done before.

All of them had executed Black's orders, which funded the team, but him and Ace went beyond the norm to please their mentor. Had done things that would make others on the team shit themselves. Definitely, they deserved extra, yet somehow, those servings always passed Kero. At first, he didn't know until Ace boasted it to his face. And then, he didn't mind because Ace was his brother and Black his father figure. Being the youngest, he thought that maybe this had been the answer to the differential of dividends. Naively, he figured going harder would defeat what he perceived as being responsible for the distinguished allocating of money they earned together. But it was to no avail. Everything remained the same besides Ace's portion, which continued to grow. And the more it grew, the more distant he made himself from the Hand and Black's influence, especially Black himself, who often claimed to be a real nigga that did real shit.

However, real niggas didn't do stuff like that. Real niggas made sure the food was put on the table and ate at the same table with niggas who had portions alike. Which wasn't the case then. Black had been eating. Mal had been eating, and Ace had as well, while the rest had only ate.

He couldn't speak for the others; they had the connects, the jukes — the mind frames to organize and keep a team above water. But he at least wanted the same as Ace, the same as Black. Hell, he knew he deserved exactly that and wouldn't settle for anything less. Fuck how long it would take. He felt he was capable of doing it also — on his own.

Him and Ace had both been taught and trained the same way, so why wouldn't he be able to run his own? Organize his own, feed his own, which day after day seemed to become more inevitable. Of course, Ace was his brother from another mother, but Ace changed and now he saw no other choice but to do the same as his fellow comrade had done with Black. The time was ripe for him to do him. For him to show niggas how it was supposed to go. To, once and for all, prove his capability of being the leader of others.

"Nigga," growled Kero, biting down on his bottom lip, "one day, you gone see how far that shit get you. Then, I want you to say that same shit."

Spain stared at him, not understanding what he was getting at. But he could clearly see that it was something on his mind, deeper than Ace's falling back. His eyes were speaking words his mouth held back. Nouns and verbs he probably couldn't put in their proper order, things that would make him watchful of his brother. "Yeah, whatever," Spain returned, acting as if he'd brushed the remark off without so much as a second thought. "It's some bullshit. But if that's how you feel, then that's you."

"What? Shhh, nigga, you acting like a nigga ain't speaking some real shit," said Kero, leaning up against the car, itching to fire up the piff. Now Spain was irking his nerves.

"Some real shit?" Spain uttered, not believing his choice of words. "Nigga, like what?" Obviously, Kero wasn't hearing himself.

"Like, say the next time some wild, crazy shit happen. What? A nigga gone ball up and leave us on stuck again."

"Leave us on stuck? Nigga, we was — and still is — making some bread. Kero, be for real. What the fuck is you talking about?" Spain had to ask, realizing whatever he was thinking, he was refusing to let it go.

"My point, lil nigga. We making some until bra start back running shit. Ion know bout the rest of y'all, but I like doing my own thing. Running my own shit. Having my own shit. Fuck letting any nigga run mines." Kero smirked, placing the blunt between his lips, firing it up.

Silence overcame the two while Kero inhaled then exhaled, letting the smoke fade into thin air. He then turned to face his young protégé. "Shawty, it's only a matter of time before a nigga got to learn how to walk on his own two feet, feel me?"

Spain looked at him, saying nothing. What could he say? His mind seemed to be made up, and one thing Ace taught him was that nothing could change a nigga's mind when it reached that point. Shaking his head, he listened to the bells of the school, instantly turning his attention toward the front of the building as it released their sole purpose for being here in the first place.

. . .

"THESE WINGS TOO MUTHAFUCKING FYE!" EXCLAIMED WHITEBOY, smashing his eleventh one while him and Ace waited in South DeKalb Mall's food court for Trigga and Dawg to show. By now, they were more than twenty minutes late.

The four of them had agreed to meet here to discuss and go over a few last details before they'd make their move on Glorified Diamonds. The food court, in their eyes, was picture perfect for the handling of just about any type of business. For one, it was always packed with people trying to get their eat on. You had those who'd sit and kick it for a while. Then, there were your new shoppers who had to come through this part of the mall just to reach the stores they intended on purchasing from. But the most attractive thing about it had been the ongoing loud noise of multiple conversations.

"They aight," returned Ace after only eating a couple of them. He hated the way the Chinese drowned them in sauce. Like they were trying to cover up the real taste of the meat's nature.

"Aight?" Whiteboy sounded like he had just flat out disrespected the food. "Man, these some of the best wings a nigga done ate in a minute."

"Nigga, please. You just greedy as fuck," responded Ace to the fake excuse he was trying to use for the way he'd been fucking them up.

"Nah. Real shit, bra, I should have been messing with these," Whiteboy told him right before choking down another one.

"Shawty, you just ain't had the ones at Hong Kong over there by North DeKalb Mall."

"What? It's in North DeKalb?" Whiteboy questioned, already logging it in his mind to pay it a visit at a later date.

"Hell nah, it sit across the street in the lil plaza next to CiCi's pizza."

"Oh." Whiteboy paused to toss a spoonful of shrimp fried rice down his throat. "We can hit that later on?"

"Nigga, later on?" Ace sounded sort of surprised. "After all that, you might not have any room." He chuckled, thinking one of those hot ass wings had touched his tongue. Glancing around, Ace watched the bad females who strolled through, shooting them a few looks like they probably gave to every other nigga that had a dollar sign spinning over his head. He'd bet his last that most of those same women who'd given him the *I'd definitely fuck with you look* were the main ones that had dudes they were the mains to at home.

That was why he wasn't really thinking about a redo to the *chick thing*. No matter how faithful a nigga was, chicks were always ready to jump on the next dick that enticed their eyes. Quite naturally, females were addicted to sex ten times more than males, and if dudes could understand that, then they wouldn't feel some type of way when she stepped out for a moment of something fresh.

Though Ace never suspected Sassy of cheating. And he still wouldn't have tripped out on her if she had. Hell, he did the most behind her back and sometimes expected the same in return. He guessed he felt exactly how a majority of society felt. Being faithful just seemed sooo… boring. That was why he'd respect a female a lot more if she just kept it real and was herself. If wifey material spoke from her aura, then good. But if whoredom was written across her fore-head, that was even better. He only wanted her to be her.

But yet and still, he tried the faithful role, and time after time, he still fell victim to the next bad bitch who was as willing as he'd been. Lust, pleasure, and passion were three feelings any individual would have a complicated time overcoming, especially if the mood was right, along with the help of a few intoxicants, which further induced the one-night stand that ensued.

Lowering his gaze, with a shake of his head, he became ashamed as Sassy vividly appeared in his mind. Visualizing her beautiful face made him hate the way he was thinking —the way he'd done her. Damn, how sorry he was for not being honest. For not being the man she more than deserved. A man who'd have never put her in a predicament that led to her demise. Every day he faulted and cursed himself for all of it. He was to blame, regardless of what others tried to convince him to believe.

It hurt to be the detriment of a perfect world. And even more after remembering the dirt he'd done while she remained faithful, honest, and loyal. If only he could take it all back. Make it different. Be something other than what he had been and was.

"Damn, baby, I'm so sorry…" he mumbled under his breath, boring into the foam tray of rice. He lost his appetite at the thought of failing the person he'd loved more than anything.

Caught up in his thoughts, he hadn't heard or paid any attention to Whiteboy, who was talking to three girls who were behind them. Ace became aware of their presence when one of them asked, "What's up with him?"

Turning his head in the direction of the voice, he saw the females, who appeared to be minors. The first girl was brown-skinned, rocking a tank top like t-shirt, a mini skirt that stopped above a pair of semi-ashy knees, which were connected to a pair of unmanicured feet in some thong sandals. What really gave him the *lil girl* impression was the gelled back ponytail on her head.

The one next to her was a little taller, wearing a Hollister shirt, with a pair of tight denim jeans, and apparently the same thong sandals as her partner. Her complexion was the lightest of the bunch, and her face was the cutest with her micro-braided hair. He might have given her a higher age range, but she was hanging with the other two. So, if she wasn't their age, then most likely her mind was.

The last girl was the shortest and chunkiest of the clique. She had chocolate skin with a fat little face. She wore an American Eagle hoodie and skirt over some black leggings. Glancing farther down her, he realized she was the one with a lil money, knowing every girl group kept that one who always paid the way for the others. On her feet were a fresh pair of burgundy Vans. And let's not forget the gold flat screens in her ears with a gold neck piece to match. Her smile was beautiful, and she still was too young. Her look said she had been the one who'd made the statement about him.

After analyzing, he gave the three a genuine smile then gave Whiteboy a look like *what the hell you got going on?*

He smiled back stupidly. "He just the quiet type. This my brother, Ace," he told them, keeping his eyes locked on him.

"Heeyyy, Ace." The chunky one waved, beating the other two to the punch.

"What up…" he returned nonchalantly, not wanting to seem in any way interested.

"You cute," she said without hesitation, giving him that look she was too young to know about.

She tripping, he thought, trying to maintain his smile and avoid the awkward look he was known for giving. "Thank you, Ma. But ion think I'm cute enough for you." He could only hope she got his drift. Ace wasn't the kind of nigga to disrespect or chump off kids. That was way below his style.

"Who? Boy, you cuter than every dude I have talked to."

"Probably." He chuckled. She was making this hard. "But not the future ones. Trust me, you gone have some real lookers." Maybe his look offered the opposite of what he wanted to achieve, so he turned his attention back to his food.

"Okay, and that is supposed to mean?"

Before he could conjure his next words, the first little girl steeped in. "Girl, that's his way of saying, 'I'm good, bitch.'" Her and the giraffe burst into laughter, but lil mama didn't find it so funny. Her feelings were hurt. Ace gave lil mini skirt a disgusted glare, yet he couldn't deny that she'd been right. But he felt she shouldn't have came off on her the way she had.

"Say," he began, already regretting what he was about to do, "what's your name?" Damn, why did he have a heart for kids?

"Lexus," she responded, giving him a, *why you wanna know now*, cold stare.

"How bout you give me your math, lil Lexus. and I hit you up later?" He watched, waited, and wanted to smile, seeing how he'd made her face light up. But he definitely admired the way she kept her composure, keeping it real ladylike.

"And when will that be, Ace?"

"When the time is right, lil mama. By the way, how old are you?" He had to ask himself why he wanted to know because he knew there would be no later to their future.

"Seventeen and a half," she spoke gleefully.

"Yeah, she the youngest of this bunch," lil mini skirt interrupted with a slight attitude, feeling the need to reveal that.

Ace could peep the jealousy emanating from her face. He smiled, ignoring her statement.

"I'ma definitely hit you bout…" He paused, glancing at the time on his phone then at Whiteboy, having the perfect date or whatever you wanted to call it in mind. "How about we link up around eight?"

"Perfect," she said, looking forward to whatever he could come up with.

Putting her number into the phone, he watched the entourage disperse into the traffic of people, wondering when and how in the hell did Whiteboy come about meeting the clique.

"Man, you don't give a fuck what you catch," said Ace incredulously, looking at his homeboy stuff the reminder of his food down.

"Who?" he let out with a full mouth.

"Who? You, nigga," Ace mocked, throwing a paper napkin at him.

Swallowing a good portion of it, he asked, "What you talking bout, shawty? Them?" He nodded his head in the direction they went.

"Nigga, you know who. The fucking three musketeers who were just over here. Stupid ass."

"Man, they came up on me with all that questioning shit. Shid…" He began smiling, still chewing. "They were choosing on you, bra." He laughed.

"Well, you can thank their choosing because *we*…" Ace emphasized, pointing a finger at himself then Whiteboy, "going to take lil shawty out tonight."

"Who?" Whiteboy acted as if he hadn't heard him right.

"You and me," Ace said slowly, so his retarded ass could fully comprehend his words.

"Man, you tripping. You trying to get a nigga cased up. And plus, I got other plans for tonight."

"Well, that shit a dub now and cased up? Nigga, we gone take her ass to Chuck E. Cheese."

Whiteboy laughed, almost choking off the last little bit of food.

"Man, you on some stupid shit. And who you supposed to be, telling me what the fuck *I'ma* do?"

"Who the fuck you think? Yo muthafucking daddy," Ace joked, knowing that line would touch a sensitive spot.

"What? Nigga, you betta watch that shit," warned Whiteboy seriously.

"Nigga, whateva. Yen talking about a bitch ass thing."

"Aight. Play with it."

"Aight what? Shawty, you just gone get punched the fuck out," Ace assured him, thinking there was going to be a time when he would really have to show him what was popping.

Whiteboy acted like he was about to laugh. "By who? Ace, you must have forgot who big bra?"

"*Lil* bra, when it came down to these," Ace replied, putting both fists up, giving him a clear view, "and you must of forgot about what happened last time?" Ace felt he had to remind him of the time when they'd put the gloves on.

Whiteboy's smirk ceased. "Nigga, yo ass got off cause I slipped. Keep popping and we gone see if you can do that shit again… Matter of fact, fuck all that. We definitely gone make some free time," he finished, wishing they had some time right now, disliking the fact that he'd let Ace get off on him one *little* time. He had to straighten his face, or this nigga would continue to brag about it.

"Say no more. Remember you asked for it." Ace laughed, realizing he'd have to tighten up. After being out of commission for so long and talking about messing with Whiteboy, he knew he would definitely have to do it more sooner than later.

Glaring, Whiteboy said nothing else. There was no need to. Whenever the opportunity presented itself, it definitely would go down. Another fifteen minutes passed before Ace heard Whiteboy say lowly, "There they go."

Turning away from the fine female he'd been making eye contact with, he glanced in the direction that Whiteboy's eyes were locked on. There was Trigga in those same Ray-Bans, walking in a way that said he could have been the owner of the mall and everything else he surveyed. Ace had to admit that the nigga had an aura about himself that spoke nothing besides the language of authority. Beside him, matching his exact pace, was another dude Ace had never seen before. From the looks of it, he sure didn't look like someone in need of a lick. The sparks from the ice on his neck danced sporadically, matching the tune of those blinging from his watch piece. With every step he took, a new form of the light show ensued.

Extra paid could have easily been pinned to dude's head, but Ace knew as well that it, mostly likely, was a front. Niggas in the city had been known for giving the appearance of a major league baller with racks galore. Yet that was the cap — to lure a person in who actually possessed a real sack then strip them of it. It was one of the oldest tricks in the game. But it was one of the most guaranteed also. People always chased after their lust, and if they weren't cautious enough, then they'd find themselves falling victim to it.

"Who that?" questioned Ace, glancing over at Whiteboy, who was watching the pair a little bit too hard.

"That's Dawg…" he said, breaking his gaze for a moment to give Ace a look that said he really needed to be on point right now.

Without another word being said, Ace's eyes switched back to the two. He understood the real meaning behind White's brief gaze.

Something wasn't right with the dude named Dawg, and whatever it was made Whiteboy seem a tad uncomfortable. Which was enough to cause Ace to become real uncomfortable.

No nigga he'd encounter with his best friend had moved him to respond the way he did. There definitely laid some form of shady shit within the guy. Whiteboy knew dude, Ace knew Whiteboy, and Ace trusted Whiteboy more than anybody else in the world. Nothing more had to be spoken or done. Ace would keep an eye on every word, action, and look Dawg said, did, and offered. Plain and simple.

"What's poppin?" exclaimed Trigga, finally reaching their table.

"What up?" returned Whiteboy with a smile as he stood on his feet. First, he dapped up Trigga then Dawg halfheartedly.

Standing himself, Ace had done the same, giving Dawg a suspicious look before halfway dapping him up. This nigga's entire vibe gave him even more reason to adhere to Whiteboy's actions. Something wasn't right.

The thing about most street niggas was that they possessed a knack for sensing when another nigga was flawed, having deeply within him some fucked up characteristics. This would always eventually lead a nigga to his own demise, all thanks to their own uncontrollable nature. This was why hittas paid attention to every single detail of another's doings, basically trying to beat time before it reached that point or worst, him ending up a victim of the ill mindset of another ill nigga. You had to play niggas close if you intended on keeping your life. Shit was real.

"I see you niggas over here fucking up some shit," chuckled Trigga, acknowledging the unburied graveyard on Whiteboy's tray.

"Word," agreed Dawg on the comment. He licked his lips before saying, "Yo, B, that shit just made me hungry. I'm about to grab some of them wings. You trying to eat?" he asked Trigga, taking a few steps toward the Chinese food stand.

"Nah, I'm good." He took a seat right across from Ace. Something within him said that Trigga sitting directly opposite of him had been intentional.

"So, what the move is, bra?" Whiteboy saw no need in wasting time. They were here to discuss business and business only.

Trigga smiled. "Shid, you already know we bout to do the damn thing on this lil play. We can't be bullshitting with it. Too much is on the line, fam." He spoke as if he was trying to hint at something unsaid.

"Already," Whiteboy told him, rubbing his hands together.

"So, what we talking about?" Ace felt the need to cut in and ask since he hadn't heard one thing about the location. He hated being in the blind.

Trigga leaned forward, removing the frames from his face. "Well, the time is going to be around ten thirty…" Clearly, Trigga was letting him know whose ball game it was. And for now, Ace would have to be fine with that.

"Ten thirty?" Ace stared him dead in the eyes, wondering who in the hell in their right mind would rob something so early in the day, a time when most people were moving to and from and a time when more police were patrolling.

"Exactly. That's the best time of any day."

"Shhh. You got to explain this." Ace was dying to know how he came to that crazy ass conclusion. Nobody he knew would ever think that ten thirty a.m. was the best time for anything besides sleep and morning sex.

"Let me ask you some'n," Trigga began, pulling his phone out. "What do you think about when you first step out of the door?"

"Doing what I had in mind before I stepped out," Ace said, trying to see exactly what this had to do with what they were talking about.

"And what do you expect?" Trigga smiled at his phone before tucking it back away. His eyes were set unwaveringly on Ace.

"Expect? Whatcha mean?" returned Ace, a little confused.

"Nigga, what do you expect to happen? You a street nigga, right?" Trigga chuckled slightly but kept his eyes as they were.

Ace guessed his staring, along with the questioning, was some kind of superior-inferior technique he used on niggas to situate who were which. The last nigga he let hold the title of superiority in his life tried to take it. So, what did he look like, letting another do the same? That was a big no-no. But he'd play his little game and let him feel how he wanted to until the time came to switch the cards on the table. "Whatever come at a nigga. I try to peep shit from a mile away," said Ace, throwing his own little hint of what he'd been thinking.

It seemed as if Trigga caught and took a liking to it.

"Exactly, exactly. Because you a street nigga and you know the things that come with this life."

"Hell yeah." Ace was still at a loss on the point he was trying to make.

"Now put yourself in the shoes of a muthafucka that's not a street nigga. A regular joe who only thinks about clocking in and out of his nine to five, unaware of all the possibilities that could take place at any given moment. You know what I'm saying? Some unexpected shit."

Silently, Ace shuffled in his seat a little, now seeing what he was getting at. Though and still, within his own mind, he felt ten thirty was crazy. Trigga might have been right about how people wouldn't be ready for something to jump off in the morning. But would that prevent them from noticing something out of the ordinary? That was the real question.

"I guess..." Ace finally retorted, accepting the fact that his mind had been set, and any alteration wouldn't be allowed.

"I know," Trigga quickly confirmed, displaying how confident he was in handling his business.

Sitting there, Whiteboy smiled at the two egos which were bound to collide. He only hoped it took place after they got the money first. "So, today, we gone check the spot out?" Whiteboy questioned before either of the two took it further.

Lying his hand flat on the table, Trigga leaned back a bit. A smirk ran across his face again as a few thoughts flew through his mind about how he and Ace would solve their differences. "Yeah. But I wanted you all to get a feel for Daw..."

Whiteboy could tell that something had snatched his full attention. Apparently something right behind them.

In unison, both of their heads swiveled backwards toward a bunch of shoppers moving about. Then they saw the foreign looking dude. A white dude — mid height, medium built —_stood erect with his eyes locked in their direction. His attire was that of a well established businessman. He wore creased slacks, a button-down coat to match the pants, and a pair of expensive looking loafers. Money spoke from the aura he possessed and even more so from the entourage which accompanied him like bodyguards did celebrities.

From the looks of it, Ace easily figured he was someone of importance. Probably mafioso. But mafioso in South Dekalb Mall? *Yeah, right!* One thing about it was that everybody wanted to appear to be somebody. And this might have been one of those times. Ace stared at the guys in the center of the group of shoppers, who began to move again with a touch of conservativeness, making it unmistakable that he held some type of authority. It was crazy how the three henchmen maneuvered around him as if waiting on an ambush. Ace continued watching closely as they moved a little bit farther.

After another moment passed, the dude broke his staring, momentarily sweeping his pupils over the scenery like he was expecting to see someone else.

Following suit, Ace scanned over the entire vicinity. He hoped to get a brief peep at whoever he'd been searching for in case some *unexpected* shit jumped off. He could see unmistakably that some kind of animosity existed between him and Trigga. Trigga's face said it all, along with the way he now clenched his jaws. His eyes narrowed, not with anger but with an intensity Ace couldn't quite define. Saying nothing, he turned his focus back to *Mr. Mafia,* who leaned slightly over, taking his attention off of them. He began whispering into one of his goon's ear.

Ace glanced over at Whiteboy, who was already looking at him. His eyes were communicating exactly what he'd been thinking. Together, they turned to Trigga, who was either mocking dude's half-hearted smile or giving him one for disrespectful purposes. Trigga's expression lightened a little. It was a look that spoke a language he didn't understand.

The fuck is going on? Ace thought, swiveling his head quickly from Trigga and back to Mr. Mafia. "What's good with Vinny?" he finally asked, refusing to be left in the blind. He wanted to be in the know on whatever the situation was or could lead to.

Trigga kept his eyes on the entourage as he told him, "Shit..." With the word, his hand slid from the table to his side. Shaking his head slowly, Trigga said, "Ain't shit going on. Let's push."

Standing with his hand clutched on his strap, he slid the chair from behind him.

Without hesitation, Ace quickly got to his feet, sending his digits for the butt of his pistol. Whiteboy's movement followed Ace's.

Reacting, the entourage swiftly went for the inside of their suit coats. It all seemed so familiar to Ace, like he had witnessed it first-hand before. At the moment though, he couldn't remember when or where, only knew that somewhere in the past, it had occurred. He could feel it.

Mr. Mafia smiled a little more, as if trying to restrain himself from bursting out into laughter, while he glanced down at his hands. He then dusted off imaginary lint, which was supposedly on the outer layer of his suit, exactly where his other hand bulged outward.

"Dawg..." Trigga said, a little above his normal voice, getting the attention of a few civilians along with Dawg's, who was unaware of what was about to take place if either of the four flinched or move the wrong way. "Let's do it." Trigga began stepping backwards. He used his eyes to let him know the reason for the rush.

Instinctively, Dawg turned his head. His mouth opened, but nothing came out once he noticed the small band of immigrants a short distance away. Instantly, his movements imitated that of Trigga's.

Keeping his eyes on them, Ace treaded backwards, wondering what Trigga continued to leave them in the blind about. However, at the moment, any briefing and conversation had no room to enter the picture. Yet and still, he wanted to know at least what the circumstances were before they popped on some muthafuckas. Or ended up in some deep shit which him and Whiteboy had the slightest clue about. But again, that would have to wait.

It couldn't have been fast enough; they made their way out of the food court, never turning their backs to them. Doing such might have been fatal. Trigga didn't seem to be the type to run from a fight. But right now, he felt threatened enough to do so.

The four became still, amusedly watching the retreat as consumers treaded around them.

Coming to a halt, Ace noticed Whiteboy hadn't moved an inch. His body was as still as their rivals were. "White..." he called out. Ace knew Whiteboy would rather deal with whatever they had on their minds. Ace wouldn't let that occur though. This wasn't their battle, even though running away was something he despised more than anything.

Whiteboy said nothing in return, only gave a quick glance backwards then back to the Italians. Reluctantly, he began taking baby steps toward Ace and them as his hand tightened around the butt of his pistol. They backpedaled to the entrance of the mall without one time showing their backs to the opposition — well, Trigga and Dawg's foes.

But doing such could be fatal when people these days were capable of anything. *Unexpected things*, like Trigga had mouthed only moments ago.

Finally reaching the sun's burning rays, Ace moved his hand from his waistline then gestured at Trigga. "Say…"

"Yo?" he quickly returned, running his retinas over the parking lot, keeping his pace as he walked in the direction of his whip.

"We need to talk."

Instantly, Trigga stopped, fixating his eyes on him. He attempted to read what laid behind Ace's eyes but quickly decided against it. Whatever was on his mind was obviously about to reveal itself.

"Here, Dawg…" Trigga dug into his pocket. "You and White follow us." He then tossed over the keys.

Before either of them had a chance to object, they heard Ace say, "The car this way." The two of them headed toward it without saying another word.

Whiteboy stood there a few more seconds, eyeing them as they continued on. He clearly understood their motive for the sudden one-on-one. Hell, he felt it was more than necessary and the only way they'd see somewhat eye-to-eye. He just hoped an understanding was meant to be gained on both sides and nothing more. The last thing he wanted was for the main objective to be missed. Whiteboy knew how Ace was and how Trigga's mouth could get. Both were too parlous to be left alone in closed quarters such as the interior of a car. Yet the thought of what would be accomplished after both personas stepped onto the same footing made it a risk Whiteboy was willing to take.

But was it a wise choice to make? He shook his head slightly while treading over the scorching black top. The success of this lick rested solely in their hands. So common ground definitely needed to be found for its sake. Or at least for Dawg's sake. Whiteboy smiled at him while inconspicuously removing the pistol from his waist. He'd keep it out of sight though accessible enough in case the two personalities found it impossible to converge on anything besides the cancelling of the other. His smile spread wider across his face as he pulled the car door open.

CHAPTER FIVE

"**A**in't no fucking way niggas did that to you… I'ma make all of them pay. I swear, bra. I'ma kill 'em all… How the fuck you get caught down bad like that? I should have been there with you that night instead of fucking with them bum ass hos… Tripping, muthafucking tripping. I'm sorry, bra. I promise I ain't gone stop till I push all their heads back. Just help me. Point me in some type of direction or give a sign. Something!" Dude stared at his reflection, the reflection of a man who'd lost someone and who was on the verge of losing something else. His mind.

It had been two days and counting since he received the news that shook his world — news that made him want to murder everybody he saw. That made him want to put the muzzle of a gun to his own temple. Three words had been the reason for it all. Everything had changed in that small instant. And nothing would be the same. His mentor, his teacher, his protector and guider. His best friend and brother had been viciously killed by somebody who could be anybody and on the same note, somebodies.

Uncertain, unknowing, and lost on all accounts fit the ramblings of his mind. He had the slightest clue as where to start his killing spree, but somewhere close were his first thoughts. He knew his brother all too well to accept the fact that he actually slipped. Big bra constantly enforced his policy on staying aware and suspicious of everything. And he was always the one to stick to his word. He led by example. Not one single time had he seen him doing anything other than that. Nah, if niggas caught him, it would have been those next to him. If not in his immediate circle, then those right at the edge of it.

These streets were cold and ruthless, strewn with the debris of conniving souls. Some would betray and cut down those they once claimed loyalty to, all for a green piece of paper — or mere envy.

Edgewood was the birthplace of his brother who continued to visit it more than anywhere else. He'd been mentored by its cruel influence and instilled with all of its treacherous ways. He grew up in the belly of the beast, enclosed by all the demonic souls which prompted its nickname, Hell's Crater.

He deeply felt those same souls were responsible for his brother's early demise. His brother was comfortable there, knew everybody, showed undeserving love to everyone regardless of their status in life. He went more than out of his way to help. Yet someone finally proved he was stupid for being so kindhearted and that they were crazy enough to try him.

However, people in the hood knew how he and his brother's team got down in the streets. His brother had a rep around the city for being a grab you, keep you, blow your brains out nigga. Then add to the fact that he had enough bread to flood a bakery, which would make the mouths being fed by that bread overprotective of him. It was hard for him to comprehend someone running down on him and not one person being in the know nor catching the backlash. Then, he knew his brother wasn't the type to go out without putting up a fight. That was just how he rocked. Straight all out, fuck the outcome.

After hearing the way his body had been found, he could see a bitch being part of the equation. That same bitch niggas remembered him exiting the club with. But if you asked him, there wasn't a ho capable of doing what they said was done. The sighting was all bad. His stomach did summersaults as he visualized the distorted face of his brother — a face which screamed of a terrible agony.

For the first time since he stepped in the bathroom, his eyes lowered from the mirror. His stomach lurched and turned at the brief thought. He needed to block out the image of the face and keep whatever was in his stomach down. Because if not, this would be the seventh time he regurgitated.

He forced a new thought to come to mind. His people were on the lookout for the girl, but that was nothing but futile, laborious work to punish those who slipped. There were a million and one bitches in the city who'd easily fit the description that had been given. So. they would search until they found her, or the bottoms of their shoes wore off. He cared less about which came first.

Chastising to the hundredth degree, he christened it. There was no way in hell they'd find a face that could match every other girls. Impossible task, he knew, but while they initiated the frivolous search, he would focus his attention on finding the real perpetrators. The ones who put the ho up to it. The same exact ones who'd have some type of knowledge of his whereabouts on the night of the murder. The knowledge which only a few dudes in their clique possessed, along with very few in the hood.

The clique became his main focus. A good starting point. The particular spot he'd been found in, again, only a few knew of. The same ones who visited it for one reason. To cop and nothing else. He couldn't vision anyone outside of his clique's members walking up to the front door and getting a friendly welcome in, especially a welcoming that wouldn't wake all of the neighbors. Things would have gotten heated and real fucking loud at his brother's place of business. But it didn't.

He quickly dismissed the notion that somebody followed him there and crept up on him. The street was one way in, one way out. Plus, his brother had a few cameras installed along his street a few years ago. He'd see any vehicle from a mile away. Whoever it was had plotted — for God knew how long — and laid on the perfect opportunity to execute, as if it all had been predestined with the good timing and the perfect execution.

But there existed one major flaw. They'd acted it out on the wrong muthafucka's brother. He'd killed numerous times. Had hunted and preyed on those who'd misunderstood his nature. He wouldn't sleep until he found her — and them. Then, he'd subject them to the most miserable, agonizing — unthought of — torment he could think of.

Rage and anger boiled within him, rising higher with every single memory of his brother. And he'd use those two emotions to fuel the fire he planned on burning the city down with.

Moving his hand from the rim of the sink, he picked the Glock nine from the bathroom's counter. He admired it for a mere second then stepped backwards, taking aim at his reflection. He caused the sight to find its mark. Right between his eyes. He stared long and hard, wondering how it would feel to experience the sear of a bullet penetrating the outer layer of his skin, sinking farther until piercing the frontal bone of his cranium. Would he feel it digging its way between the material of brain matter until it exited through his occipital bone?

Nothing could explain the way he felt on the inside. Twenty-five years of running side by side with the one person who gave a damn about you. Then, in an instant, having somebody snatch them away forever. Denying you that right to say goodbye for the last time. His eyes teared up; his hand trembled slightly. He wanted to calm his screaming emotions but could muster no reason to. He was alone in the bathroom. Alone in the world. A lot had taken place over the previous months. Losses on top of losses, of both money and homies, but the death of his older brother had taken the cake.

He'd been strong, enduring all of it. Every bit, even this when he first got word of it. Now though, standing and staring, it seemed as if his entire world was about to crumble if he continued to hold in the pain which ate at his very soul. Tearing away every shred of what he'd been made of. Anguish spread across his face. A tear followed by another one broke from a single eye. He loathed crying, something he had avoided until now, but this was too much, and he didn't care. Shit hit homebase. Shit had gotten real.

CHAPTER SIX

"And where are the happily married going, for let's see—" Alex smiled as his eyes rolled toward the ceiling femininely. He leaned over the counter, taking a sip from the coffee he'd been nursing for the last ten minutes. "Their third honeymoon?"

"Stop it. It's only been one of those. The other two have been, what I'd like to call, experiences of the universe's sexual U.N.I.T.," Marsha said, savoring the memory of those sexual escapades.

"Okay, bitch, and that means?" Alex questioned, giggling along with Alethea.

"Well…" Marsha began, placing her hands on her hips, thinking the explanation of her 'made up' acronym was about to trip them both out. "The universe's sexual Unusually Nasty Incessant Therapy."

"What?" laughed Alethea, wondering if she'd heard right.

Alex put his coffee mug down quickly. "Oh, girl, I just love your imagination." He smiled, hugging her like she'd made his day.

Unable to control her laughter, Alethea waited on Alex to do his regular, uttering the first thing that came to mind. That was something she knew would be hilarious. This had been part of their normal routine prior to opening up for business. It was always good — in her opinion —_to share a morning laugh before an arduous day of dealing with the stubborn, arrogant, yet very wealthy assholes that somehow always found a new way of making her day irritable and extra-long. She constantly had to remind herself to maintain her composure if she wanted to keep a job and its very appreciative benefits. But it was at an aggravating price.

Alethea had been working for Glorified Diamonds for a little over a year and a half. Their Amsterdam Walk location was her third transfer within the ten-store franchise and hopefully her last. The previous locations had taken a toll on her, which left her distressed and too uncomfortable with the industry of jewelry. Then, let's not forget about robberies. The mental stress of those situations and the fact that it could happen again was becoming too much for her to bear. Way too much to deal with.

"Now tell me, girl," Alethea heard Alex say, springing her from the brief reverie. Bringing her head up, she saw Marsha was placing one finger to his lips.

"No, Alex, don't go there…" Before she could finish, Brian, the store's security guard, came from the back.

"Thank you, Lord. And Marsha, please don't let him go nowhere near there," Brian said, spacing his last words out, adding a small chuckle.

Giving him an icy glare, Alex smacked his teeth. "Well, we should because our exotic conversations is about as near as you going to get to the real thing Brian."

Brian stopped in his tracks. Alethea was more than ready for the show. Smiling brightly, Brian turned to him. "So, let me guess, your definition of what the *real thing* is you feeling the real *flesh* of another man?" he finished with a mocking laugh, beginning to step off again.

Alex's eyes narrowed on him. "Are you sure you want to go there?" He crossed his arms, conjuring his next remark.

"What? You gonna snap finger me to death?" He chuckled, imitating the way drags did it, snapping his fingers while he waved his arm back-and-forth.

Both Alethea and Marsha laughed, preparing themselves for the unexpected. Dropping his head a bit, Alex's lips twisted into a smirk. "Speaking of snapping, you sure did when I turned you down on this *real thing*," he finished, adding emphasis.

"Uhhh…" Alethea was ineffable. Marsha covered her mouth in total shock. The words had caught both women off guard and, at the same time, caused Brian's face to go pale then quickly turn into a bright red glow.

Alethea was astounded by the fact that Brian might have actually been gay. Then, on top of that, he had made a secretive pass at Alex who, obviously, declined it for real. It became more amusing after she ran it through her mind again. Brian was one of the few white males that she actually found sort of attractive — in some ways. His charisma was great with an appealing sense of humor. He always knew the right words to say when you were feeling down and out, without trying to hook up with you afterwards. Unlike a majority of the typical dudes.

Now thinking about it, she realized that Brian hadn't made a move on her or Marsha. But then again, maybe he made a pass at Marsha. She never thought to ask. Yet now, after hearing the shocking revelation of the day, she'd be sure to ask her when they took their lunch break. Together.

Brian stared him down hard, like at any second he was going to kill their gay manager. Alethea hadn't ever seen him display a face like this before. Brian was the laid-back type, always keeping a cool composure, no matter what slick comment Alex shot his way. This was unusual, which caused Alethea to believe that the statement had some truth to it. "Talking about some *Jerry Springer* stuff," she muttered sotto voce, shaking her head, finding it all entertainingly disgusting.

Obviously, Marsha caught the menacing glare as well, which was probably why she quickly filled some of the space between the two of them. "Brian," she started, stretching out her arms as if she'd been waiting on a big hug, "it's time to open up." Laughter was on the verge of spilling from her, but she knew that would only make matters worse.

A moment or two later, Brian finally removed his blazing pupils from Alex, giving Marsha a look that said things were far from over. He then proceeded in stepping toward the entrance. Twisting her head around, Marsha gave Alethea a quick, *unbelievable* look. Then, she swiveled slightly toward Alex, softly pushing his shoulder as she passed him.

Alethea smiled, thinking break time would be one to remember. The store was quiet. No customers had come in since Brian had unlocked the doors, which was about forty minutes ago. It seemed as if all of them were holding their tongues and breaths until break time.

Brian was sitting on a stool. He was staring through the front window at whatever would keep him from facing the sudden reality which found its way through the opening of Alex's lips.

Alex was leaning over the counter, cleaning a few pieces of jewelry. Every now and then, he'd peep over at Alethea with a smirk on his face. Marsha — the whole time — had been forming silent words with her mouth until she finally got tired of that and picked up a *People* magazine.

Alethea was sitting there, checking out the scenery and texting her new friend, who she quickly found to be *not so interesting*. The atmosphere spoke in tones yet remained quiet and calm. Mute. Then, the bell rang from a customer pulling the front door open.

"Thank God..." Alethea uttered lowly to herself, never thinking she'd be so glad to see a customer. Boredom was something she hated more than these annoying buttholes and grown ass brats. The past minutes had been an ass kicker for her. She watched the light complexion guy, whose dress attire was a mixture of urban with a touch of conservativeness. He had on a pair of Dolce and Gabbana shades that were a little too big for his face. The guy strolled in like he was the coolest man on the planet. It was ridiculous enough to grab all four pairs of eyes.

As he made his way over toward Alex and Marsha's side of the store, she noticed that he didn't quite fit into the category of the usual upper class shoppers Glorified Diamonds attracted. He exuded the aura of a *wannabe*, and she totally knew that *wannabes* most likely lacked the necessary funds to actually purchase from the five-star jewelry distributor. But here he was.

"Welcome to Glorified Diamonds..." Alex greeted the patron femininely. The dude smiled, turning his gait toward the hospitality.

Impossible. A gay parade must be going on today or something? Alethea wondered, shooting Marsha, who definitely had to be thinking the same exact thing, a quick glance. Her look said it all. Alethea then glanced over at Brian, who glared at the two. No. He was probably sick to his stomach. But then again, maybe jealousy was emitting from him.

The inside joke tickled her. She spun back, watching Alex and the stranger, who were now engaging in small talk. Studying dude's features from head to toe, she could see he had a little taste in dressing and was color coordinated. You could assume he had the potential of a fashion model. His build resembled that of an athlete, tipping closer to the figure of a boxer, which she admitted she had a thing for. It was the way they exhibited their masculine prowess on one another. This always made her moist between the legs and horny to the core. A *thing* he might have been capable of causing had he not possessed whatever it was encouraging him to be a down low brother.

Too bad, Alethea thought, dropping her eyes to the sound of plastic vibrating on glass. Another message was coming through on her touchscreen. Reading the first part instantly brought a smile to her face. Again, the sound of the front door's bell went off. Before she could lift her head, the words, "Get the fuck up!!!" resonated viciously across the room.

Instantly, her heart rate increased, pounding harder and harder. *Unbelievable.* She watched Brian get smacked to the floor by another unexpected visitor with a hat on. "Oh, God..." Alethea mumbled to herself as the individual waved the pistol from Brian's bleeding face toward them.

"Ah!" She cringed at the loud shriek that came from across from her. Marsha was somewhere screaming. Alex was holding the side of his face, slouching backwards on the desk behind him. The boxer quickly climbed over the glass case, gripping Alex by the neck while aiming at Marsha's beautiful, blonde head.

Alethea's body stiffened at the horrific scene unfolding before her very eyes. She could hear Brian letting out a painful moan while the

sound of metal slamming into his skull resonated. She wanted to run —
begged her body to do something. But it wouldn't even attempt to
budge.

Marsha, though, tried to do what looked like the standing *worm*,
but her movement quickly ceased. Mr. *Wannabe* gripped her hair and
brutally slung her into the wall.

"Marsha!" Alethea gasped. Marsha's head cracked and dented the
drywall. Stunned and still stuck, she watched her co-worker crumble to
the floor. Then, she heard the words, "Bitch, get to the muthafucking
back." The guy in the hat, who'd hit Brian, was now holding him by
his hair, dragging him.

Neither him, nor the *wannabe,* had been the one to utter the words.
Alethea must've been too caught in the moment not to hear the stupid
little sound of the bell. Turning in the direction of the voice, she immediately saw the orifice of a pistol. Beyond that, another guy in a hat
gave her the meanest look she'd ever encountered. Her knees buckled,
on the verge of causing her to have a one-on-one with the floor. She
could only pray things went as usual — them getting what they came
for without her being harmed. Yeah, this would be the last time she
worked for Glorified Diamonds.

"Everything is going good..." confirmed Lucky, who was very
relaxed, leaning back in the reclining chair directly across from Paul.

"Great," returned Paul, taking a light pull from his Columbian
cigar. "Have you spoken with the Yankees?" he asked before making
eye contact with his representative, Angelo.

"I'm still waiting on a response, but Felix hinted that all was well.
Well, as long as we get, you know, the *situation* taken care of."

Paul exhaled, aware of exactly what *situation* he was referring to.
He'd been trying to figure out the *how* in getting it done without
anything leading back to him or any member of his organization. It
would be bad for business and definitely very harmful to the family on
a multitude of levels. That alone made the matter delicate, meaning
he'd have to acknowledge most of the sensitivities surrounding it. This

was why he was here now. He needed to know what those in New York were thinking, feel them out a little before he handled it.

However, before this little chat, Paul had come up with a few ideas, one being the recruitment of out of towners. But that wouldn't look good in the eyes of the other families. Such an action would do nothing more than making him appear dependent on the others and unable to operate his very own, newfound branch of the Manterio family.

Paul had been over the Atlanta chapter of the family for a little over six years and had nonetheless earned a great amount of respect. So, he couldn't just let it be diminished because he failed to stand up to the expectations of what he'd become —_a boss. Now came the time for him to show those who wanted him to come up short, like a few, fellow members of the board, who were dying to replace him with their personal favorite ass kisser, Asher.

Only a few problems had occurred since he'd become top dog. Yet none of them compared to the situation at hand. The drastic event itself had ignited a scorching fire under everyone's asses. And it wouldn't subside until the lost property was returned.

Paul had only discovered the identities and locations of those responsible a couple of months ago. But Paul, being Paul, wanted the money first; then, he'd personally send them to hell. Now, his only objective was revenge, given how much pressure the Yankees applied. He could understand their feelings —_he'd feel the same way if his own son had been on the receiving end of that fatal blow.

"In due time…" muttered Paul almost inaudibly, taking another pull from the cigar. "Any word on…" A knock on the door forced him to swallow the rest of his question. When meetings like this one were taking place, there were to be no interruptions. Unless it was vital.

He could only wonder about the reason for the disturbance. *What now?* he thought, glancing down at his chrome Bolivia for the time. "Still early," he mumbled under his breath then watched as Frankie appeared from the other side of the door. "Boss, another one just got popped," Frankie whispered into his ear.

Paul smirked, sweeping his eyes over his associate. He remained calm after hearing the news. He didn't have to hear the entire details.

His fourth commercial business had been robbed. Right now, however, wasn't the time to waiver from the conversation they were having either though.

"So, any word on our runner?" Paul asked, needing to finish the meeting with all the facts. Then he would figure out how to deal with the unfortunate robbery, especially since he already had knowledge of who the perpetrators were. He could only smile.

"FUCKING RIGHT!" EXCLAIMED TRIGGA AS THEY STARED ADMIRINGLY at the small mountain of jewels on the table. The move they'd pulled on Glorified Diamonds had ended up being a lot more than originally expected. There sat before them a little over three million in iced out pieces in exchange for a couple minutes of work which, surprisingly, had worked.

Never would Ace have thought about sticking up any type of commercial establishment. And never had he, besides the first one him and Whiteboy had done so long ago. Which really wasn't a *real robbery*. Yet after witnessing the proceeds of today's lick, he began rethinking his career choice. This had been a lot quicker, and they had made the equivalent amount that would have taken at least two weeks or more to make when he'd been pushing dope through the streets.

Yeah, it was a crazy idea at first, definitely after hearing what they'd have on as a disguise. Then there was how they'd rush in and straight ransack the place like wild wild west bandits. It was insane, but it worked as planned without even the slightest trouble from the law. Well, not as of right now anyway.

Ace glanced over at Trigga, who was to the left of him, picking up jewelry one piece at a time, marking down the numbers attached to them. Whiteboy sat across from Trigga, doing the same. And Dawg was directly opposite of Ace. He was twisting up some gas. Ace couldn't help but to muse over what the final total would come out to once they were finished. He needed the result to be in the six figures or more bracket, especially when Trigga had assured him that he already had some people lined up to cop it all from them. Though half was only what the people were willing to pay. Hell, he already knew that much. Who in their right mind would pay full price for some hot shit? Nobody he knew or could think of. So, the results — again —needed to be real high. And if the numbers weren't in the range of his rough estimation, then he figured he'd just knock Dawg and Trigga off, limiting it to a two-way split.

But I don't know the purchasers... yet... Leaning back in his chair, Ace stared at the ice mountain, loving the way it glistened, almost resembling ice falling right out of a faucet of diamonds. A ring sat at the right edge of the pile, gaining his full attention. It was almost like it had called his name and stopped in that particular spot for his sight and no one other than him. Reaching, he picked it up and began studying some of the customized details. It had been cut uniquely with accurate precision, speaking eloquently by its design. The clear, mesmerizing stone in the center was beautiful, reminding him of the only thing more precious than it. Sassy.

Damn, how the thought made him want to place it on her finger. His all in all. The one person that made his life seem complete. But in all honesty, marriage was the furthest thing from his mind when him and Sassy first got serious. Though, as time continued to progress, with him paying more attention to how happy married couples were at times, he became a little curious about it. And he somehow felt it had been what she wanted without her having to say so. He often sensed her odd actions when they'd encounter couples engaging in regular activities of the married life — things that were normal but exercised with a little more elatedness and meaning.

Obviously, a thing laid within the midst besides attraction and a presence of lust — something blessed, of value and merit. Him and Sassy belonged together, and their relationship already contained the qualities of marriage without the exchanging of vows. But one day, after overhearing a conversation between her and Latoya, one that surprised him, he decided it was time to ask that question every girl wanted to hear and faithfully commit himself to her once the bonds were wielded and the knot was tied.

But he was stripped of that chance when she'd deserved it.

Deserved to be loved, to be faithful too. To be married to the one man she felt could satisfy her every need. They said you never truly appreciated someone until they were gone, and once gone, that appreciation forever remained lost within the realm of should ofs, a place where nothing could ever be regained.

"Yo, B…" Ace heard Dawg say, springing him back from where he didn't need to be at the current moment. He looked up, presenting a slight smile, but said nothing.

"You good?"

"Yeah," Ace quickly told him, spinning the ring a bit between his fingers.

"Maybe, but you was just looking as if you needed some of this." Dawg smirked, waving the blunt horizontally. Before Ace responded, Trigga spoke without lifting his eyes from the task at hand.

"No smoking while doing business." His words were decisive, a little over authoritative.

"What?" Dawg huffed, giving him an awkward look as if he hadn't heard him right. But he had. "Nigga, you two the ones doing the adding. Me and dude just sitting here. Bored. So, you both keep up the good work and let me and my mans do us," he finished, scooting his chair back from the table, nodding his head at Ace.

Ace felt the same way. He definitely needed something to ease his mind. Plus, he wanted to show Trigga that he didn't run everyone and everything. Ace stood from the table, placing the ring off to the side, away from the pile. "Say," he said, only getting Whiteboy's attention, "don't add this with the rest. Just knock it off my cut."

Whiteboy gestured *okay*. Trigga didn't look up but said, "Aight." Whiteboy stopped, glancing over at the piece he'd mentioned then up at Ace curiously.

"What, nigga?" smiled Ace, knowing that Whiteboy was going to think of every possibility besides what he actually intended on doing with the ring. That alone would be enough to keep his mind busy for days.

Smoking the weed in silence, Ace stood on the back deck, geeked the fuck up, trying to remember anything he could think of. The gas had him kind of off balance yet still in tune with his surroundings. As long as he stood still. Every time he moved, it ended up being like the whole damn place was shifting. It had him fucked up for a second, but he knew he was dumb high and tripping. Though it felt too real to continue to test the water. *Man, I hope this shit don't fall in.* Ace laughed at the thought. Most definitely, he was tripping. Hopefully.

"What's good?" Dawg asked, turning back toward Ace. He'd been in space, high as hell too.

"Nothing, inside joke. Man, I'm higher than a muthafucka." His words caused both of them to release a chuckle. "This shit got a nigga scared to move."

"Yo," Dawg said, gripping the parapet tightly, "nigga, I thought this bitch was about to cave in. I was just in space trying to figure out how I'ma get off this shit if it do." They both laughed harder, neither moving an inch from their current places.

"Oh, best believe if this muthafucka do, it's gone bring yo ass back to Earth asap." Ace continued laughing, gazing up at the stars above. Only if he could be amongst them.

"Word! That lil piff was just the beginning of the celebration. We get this paper, we got to ball out one time at least," Dawg said, thinking of his long-time ritual. An ol school cat had taught him this long ago, saying, "If you take it from the people, then you got to give some back. And what better way to do it than splurging?" That was exactly what he'd been doing ever since.

"I'm definitely with that," Ace agreed, feeling like what better way was there to welcome him back into the life.

"Trill's-trill's. It should be a nice little piece of cake. I'm even thinking about keeping me a few pieces myself." Dawg paused briefly, rubbing his eyes. "By the way, I'm not trying to be all in your business or nothing, but you thinking about wifey 'n somebody?" Dawg asked curiously.

Ace continued to stare upwards into the darkness of the night's sky, thinking how was this nigga not trying to get into his business with a question like that. Bringing his head down, he looked over at him. "Something like that. What, you thinking about some'n similar?"

"Who?" coughed Dawg, followed by a chuckle. "Man, hell no. The only way I'm going to marry a bitch is if she playing in the major leagues with the money. Like that girl, Oprah."

"That girl, Oprah…" mocked Ace with a chuckle.

"Word. There's no way I'ma settle for a bitch in need like I am." He laughed.

"I feel that."

"So, you and your girl ready to make that big move?"

"My girl dead." Ace let it fall flatly from his lips, wondering what his next question would be since his business was out there now.

"Damn…" began Dawg lowly, uncertain if he was for real or not. But no nigga he knew of would play like that. "Sorry to hear that, b…"

"It's good." Ace lifted his eyes back to the heavens. He wished his words weren't true. But since they were, he wanted to be up there with his angel.

"I'm not trying to get in your video, but…"

Ace cut him short. "But you still got questions." He tried not to sound disrespectful about it, but this wasn't a conversation he was willing to have with a nigga he barely knew.

Dawg stared at him, understanding where he was coming from with the remark. He'd probably be the same way had the shoe been on the other foot. "Son, don't think a nigga being nosey and shit. I just like to know the type of nigga I'm dealing with, especially if we gone be pulling more moves together."

"More moves together?" Ace repeated as if his retort had been a question. How or why would he figure that something as such was possible?

"Yeah. Shid, I liked the way you and ya boy moved. It was real right. So, again, I like to know who I'm fucking with to make sure it's mutual respect, especially on the money tip. You know, without the extra shit." Dawg seemed as if he'd sobered up. He was eyeing Ace closely.

"Nah, ain't nothing extra on dis side of the fence. I'm bout one thing, paper. And I'm pretty sure ya homie told you all there was to know about me."

Dawg nodded his head, confirming. "Yeah. He told me a little something. But what's an outside opinion when you can hear it from the mouth of the man himself?"

Ace ignored the philosophical shit. "A little something like what?" Ace wondered what was about to fall from his mouth as to the description of his past or present — or both.

"Nothing really but that a nigga tried you on some other shit and that you rolled 'em. The nigga's name was..." Dawg tilted his head backwards a bit, trying to remember as he snapped his fingers.

Ace finally said, "Black."

"Word, Black. What was up with dude?"

"What you mean?" *Is this an interrogation?* Ace had to ask himself.

"Like the type shit that nigga was on. Word was that he had it because he fucked over everybody in his vicinity."

Ace smirked because he'd hit the nail right on the head. "Shid, ion know. I wasn't really fucking wit holmes like that." Ace now wanted to know why he was interested in Black. He hadn't known him personally, and Black was six feet deep. And even if he let Dawg know everything about him, it wouldn't serve a real purpose. Or would it?

"Oh..." was all Dawg uttered in return. Odd, there was no question.

"But why you asking me bout a nigga I bodied?" Ace wanted to see what he actually knew since he previously insinuated that he'd popped him, even though the statement was to the contrary.

Dawg began scratching the back of his head. "Don't take it the wrong way, my dude. You know I had my own little shit going on with du..."

Ace interrupted before he could finish. "Like what?" He had to hear this. A connection between him and Black? Really? What a coincidence. Who would have thought.

"I owed dude a bit of the same thing you served him."

"Oh, yeah?"

"Word. Dude fucked around and bodied my fam some years ago. I was gone repay the favor. But you beat me to the punch." He chuckled after his last few words.

Bodied his family? Ace wondered who he was referring to as *fam.* And some years ago? Could have been anybody at the rate Black was sending niggas to early graves. The dirt wouldn't even have settled on one person before another one had to be buried.

"Who was your fam?" Ace questioned suspiciously, thinking he probably wouldn't know them. Yet at the same time, he might. He'd put down quite a few niggas on behalf of his former leader — some years ago — and one of them just might so happen to be his people. It now looked as if it was coming together. And if he had, then Dawg would be reunited with them.

"You might know him. Lil stupid ass nigga by the name of Kay."

Kay, a name he knew all too well. It rang in his head, bringing back vivid memories of how he'd played Black and how down bad he'd caught Ace. Ace stared at Dawg incredulously, trying to remember if he'd ever heard Kay mention him before. He couldn't be sure. It was exactly what Dawg had said. Some years ago.

Clandestinely, Ace's hand went to his pistol. He was high still but not enough to let this nigga catch him off guard.

"You knew him?" Dawg asked, not catching the surprised look on Ace's face when he spit the name out.

Ace watched him closely, trying to read his face in the dim lighting for any signs of aggression. There was no telling what he actually knew. "I knew 'em a lil bit." There was no reason to lie. However it played out, that was just what it was.

"Really?" uttered Dawg nonchalantly, like he already knew that much.

Ace smiled, preparing for whatever this nigga had on his mind. His hand was under the edge of his shirt. "Why Black knock 'em off?" asked Ace, acting ignorant yet trying to focus. The high had him discombobulated, only not enough to miss any funny move this nigga might have pulled.

Dawg glanced over the balcony into the darkness, rubbing the palm of his hands together. "They say he did some grimy shit. One thing about Kay, he only dished out what was handed to him." He paused, putting his eyes back on Ace. His hands dropped to his pockets.

"Niggas say that the nigga, Black, was definitely the type to dish out shit. So the shit Kay did was nothing but a *small* repayment for the shit he was taking."

It became apparent to Ace that he might have actually knew what had gone down with the situation and could possibly have knowledge of his role within it all. It didn't make sense though. Why was he asking or telling him? Out of all people. He couldn't comprehend it. "Oh, so, you know what happened?" Ace's hand gripped the butt of the gun.

Dawg stared a second, as if expecting some other reaction than the one he responded with. It was for Ace to tell. "Word. I helped him execute the shit."

His words sent Ace spiraling back to that night. Beginning at Libra, when some dude ran down on him and Tay. Spraying bullets toward both of them. Then there was the spot where Tank was sprawled out across the floor, dead. Both of these events had been too crazy for his young mind. They were his first witnessing of how there was no such thing as *one way* to this street shit. Anybody was capable of getting it.

Ace remained silent. He wanted to know what part he'd played in the whole scheme. *Was he the one who flatlined Tank? Or did he just assist in stripping the work from the spot? Maybe he'd been the one who'd left holme out to dry at the edge of the club's parking lot?* Questions ran through his mind, bringing him almost to the point of really not wanting to know. Things were different then. There were things he couldn't understand besides his feelings. That was why he needed the answers which Dawg obviously had.

Ace offered a fake chuckle. "Boy, stop. You telling me you pulled a move on the almighty Black?"

"Word."

Word, Ace thought, not believing that this nigga was stupid enough to tell a nigga some shit like that. A nigga he didn't even know existed until a few days ago. A nigga who fucked with them other *boys*, who'd lost their lives that night. Damn, his words had fallen upon the wrong ears. "You hell now," said Ace, keeping his composure. His mind began to plot on how Dawg was about to die — and possibly Trigga too if he felt some type of way bout it.

"He was hell. If he would have been taking care of his soldiers, things wouldn't have went the way they did," Dawg said.

Ace couldn't argue with that truth. Black had a knack for fucking over every nigga he came into contact with in some form or another. That had been the only way he knew how to interact with others. "Man, you sure you didn't know none of them other niggas?"

"Nobody besides Kay. So, how long was you rocking with dude?" Dawg asked, reverting back to the beginning of the conversation. Ace knew it was a little too late for that. But he'd let him play around if that was what he chose to do. He wasn't wasting anybody's time but his own.

"Not that long. But hold that thought. I gotta piss right quick." Ace smirked, moving toward the patio's door.

"Ahhhh, shit. Shake this shit," Ace coached himself, splashing the cold water against his face. This had been the fourth time. Then another one. He stared at his reflection, pondering about how he would do Dawg. Not because he'd hit Black's spot but because of the lives that were taken due to the robbery he'd helped — in his words — execute. Tank and Ace were real cool, close on a brotherly basis —just nowhere near as close as him and Tay were. To Ace, Tay was like Whiteboy in a sense. Crazy, ridiculous, and reckless at times but always dependable and loyal. No matter what the case was, he never wavered in supporting Ace, and it was mutual. He was the one Ace could turn to when he needed a pair of ears to bear his venting, which was the only way — he said — he could clear his mind, alleviating the mountains of stress from his chest.

At times, Ace felt alone and lost in a world of chaos with no one to confide in. No one to help calm the agony searing into the depth of his soul. Then there was Tay, who'd never spoken two words to him until a certain situation occurred. It left him desolate. This was when they became as close as brothers. "You'll never be forgotten, my nigga.

Oh," Ace smirked, "and be waiting on this nigga cause he on his way to you." Pulling the pistol from his waistline, Ace ran his eyes over the surface once. Then, he snatched the slide, launching the bullet into the head which would be for the revenge of a fallen comrade.

"Yo, b, how long before y'all finish?" Ace heard Dawg ask as he made his way back up the hallway.

Trigga didn't even lift his head. "You see all these pieces? So, you tell me."

Ace stood there a moment, staring at the back of Dawg's head. He wondered how long it would take for the hot slug to penetrate his skull. Then, he glanced over at Whiteboy, who was staring at him with an expression as if he knew exactly what was on his mind. Offering a smirk, he went to the chair he'd previously sat in.

"Say, Trigga, ya man turnt up, ain't he?" Ace smiled, taking his seat, stealthily bringing the gun from his pants pocket, keeping it out of everyone's sight.

Trigga hunched his shoulders then continued to jolt down numbers.

Gazing at Trigga then Ace with his glazed eyes, Dawg let his eyes linger on Ace a little longer, suspiciously. He had perceived the slickness in his words but said nothing. He was too high to make something of it.

Ace stared back, musing over if this nigga had ever thought about dying like he was about to —_because of his mouth. The Bible said, "Guard thy eyes and mouth from seeing and speaking the wrong things." Clearly, Dawg wasn't a churchgoing person or a nigga who understood how not to say shit that wasn't necessary.

"Say, Dawg…" began Ace, shooting Whiteboy a quick glance. He then placed his eyes back on Dawg as his hand tightened around the handle of the steel. Dawg's mouth remained shut. The only movement he made was his head bobbing back-and-forth.

"That nigga you say you popped at Black's spot… His name was Tank." Within that very instant, Ace swung the pistol over the table. He steadied the muzzle while the sight aligned with Dawg's face. The movement was so swift that Trigga hadn't caught hold on what was going on until the gunfire erupted. Three repetitive shots. Rapidly, one followed behind the other. The first one found its way under his eye socket. The other two launched in the depths beyond his forehead.

Quickly, Ace sprang from his seat, grabbing the collar of Trigga's t-shirt, leaving no time for him to react. Roughly, he shoved the strap into his face.

"Wait, bra!" shouted Whiteboy, jumping to his feet, surprised at how swiftly Ace had executed Dawg and was on the verge of doing the same to Trigga. Whiteboy looked at Trigga —_then Ace again — as he spoke. "Shawty already know what's poppin."

Finger caressing the trigger, Ace glared down at who was to be his next victim then back at Whiteboy. He was confused. How the fuck could he know anything about what he was doing when he'd conjured it up alone? There hadn't been any time to consult with anything outside of his very own mind. So, unless Trigga knew how to read minds, there was no way he could've known. "How you figure he knew I was going to burn his homie? Nigga, you didn't even know…" Ace grumbled, wondering what was on Whiteboy's mind to make him assume something like that.

"Nah, nigga, you didn't till a few minutes ago," snarled Trigga through clenched teeth, sweeping his eyes to Whiteboy's.

"What, nigga?" growled Ace, forcing the gun harder against his temple.

"Bra, chill!" barked Whiteboy.

"Chill! Nigga, how you know this nigga ain't gone try some slick shit? I got to do this nigga too. You tripping, nigga."

Trigga began to smile. "On some real shit, shawty, you probably got a few more seconds to keep this shit up before I start to feel some type of way bout this whole situation."

Ace couldn't believe this nigga's audacity in his current position. Out of all the things in the world, he had the nerve to think that Ace would give a fuck about him feeling a type of way. Now, besides that of doing his partner, this was enough reason for him to do what he intended. He wanted badly to show him what pride got a nigga when messing with the wrong nigga. And for some odd ass reason, Whiteboy was insisting that he didn't, which wasn't the best friend he knew. He had been the one always down for the murder show.

Ace glared at Trigga, releasing his shirt before taking a step backwards. Yet he kept the pistol aimed at his temple, less than three inches away from his flesh. "White, on some real shit, you better have a good reason why he shouldn't be racing that nigga to hell," Ace finished, nodding his head at the lifeless body of Dawg. His finger was itching to rearrange Trigga's mental as well.

Trigga lifted his eyes. "Ace, shawty, only if you knew. Now I'ma brush that lil statement off and give you a chance — or rather two chances..."

Ace smirked, unable to help himself. This dude was on the shit end of the stick with a bullet ready to tear into his skin. But here he was, giving a nigga *chances*. He either had to be crazy or very death struck.

"Okay, either one, you put down the strap and listen to how I knew this shit was gone play out between you and the departed. Or two, you dead me, of course with the exception of me hitting you as well..." Trigga paused, dropping his retinas down toward his lap. He leaned backwards a little to reveal the gun his hand gripped which, if fired, would definitely destroy Ace's genitals. A smile stretched across his face as he uttered his next words. "Then my niggas run in here and clear the whole spot out."

It seemed almost simultaneous. Right when the words had left his lips, the sound of car doors being slammed resonated. *Oh, he think he got all the sense*, Ace thought, more than ready to take his *chances*. It now appeared to be setup. Shooting Whiteboy a quick glance, he weighed his options. Something was wrong with this entire picture. Coincidences were possible, but them occurring in this lifestyle were slim to none, especially in a situation as this one. He'd only moments ago down badded Trigga's homie, or whatever he was to him, with Trigga, seconds later, claiming that he knew he would. Then, out of the blue, niggas pulled up outside, right before he was about to dead Trigga. Setup was written all over it, but what made it seem kind of otherwise and crazy was that Whiteboy sat there like everything was all good. Either White had lost his marbles or Ace had missed a whole lot of shit.

"Please, nigga, who's to say you and whoever outside won't knock us off anyway?" questioned Ace, suspiciously eying Trigga down for the smallest sign of deceptiveness. Surely, if he caught a glimpse of any, his choices would be limited to one.

"Ace, just trust me, bra," growled Whiteboy, praying that he'd listen. However though, if he didn't, he was fully prepared to blaze it out with his brother.

Ace stared White in the eyes for a moment, hesitating a bit before finally lowering his pistol.

Please let him be right, was all he could think of as knocks from the door reverberated into his ears.

CHAPTER SEVEN

"Everything is so crazy without you, baby. It's like the more I try to live for us, the harder it gets. Not being able to talk to you and hold you. I only got the memories of what we had to dwell on. Memories that are sometimes hard to bear." Ace glanced down at the tombstone which belonged to the love of his life. Visiting Sassy's grave had evolved into a sacred ritual, a solemn pilgrimage that he went on twice a week without fail. This little secluded lot of the earth had transformed into their sanctuary, a hallowed ground where memories intertwined with grief. It was his refuge, a haven where he could untangle the knots of his thoughts and unburden his weary heart. Amidst the silent whispers of the wind and the solemn stillness of the graveyard, he found solace. Here, amidst the somber gravestone, he sought asylum from the relentless demands of reality, seeking respite from the gaping void left by her absence.

In this place of quietness, he found himself grappling with the stark emptiness that pervaded his existence — a void that only her memory could fill. Amidst the crumbling remnants of time, his love for her stood unwavering, a beacon of light in the darkness of his grief. Each visit was an arduous pilgrimage, a journey through the labyrinth of his emotions as he navigated the delicate balance between remembrance and despair.

However, amidst the sorrow and longing, he found moments of peace, listening to the sound of her spirit that whispered through the veil of mortality. For him, this sacred ground was not merely a resting place for her physical form but a sanctuary where the essence of her soul lingered, offering him fleeting moments of communion with the beloved departed.

Damn, he missed her so much. The ache of her absence was a constant irritation, an ever present shadow which haunted his every step. How many countless nights had he wished he could exchange his reality for the one next to her? To be next to his love would be more than enough to satisfy that burning desire within him. To reunite with the other half of his heart. His life.

"The other day..." he began, forcing a small chuckle to break from between his lips. "I was thinking about that time when I came out of the shower and caught you sniffing my boxer briefs..." Ace laughed a bit at the memory with his chin dropping to his chest. "Man, you should of seen your face. You swore a nigga up and down that you wasn't. But baby, the way you was looking said it all. And what about that time when you was mad at me because I was late picking you up? Then we started arguing, and you went to grabbing the steering wheel while I was driving, like you was ready to kill us both. Gurl, that's when I realized that you wasn't just playing crazy. Yo ass shot out."

After another brief laugh, Ace closed his eyes. The morning breeze glided across the top of his head and the surface of his skin. Tears began to pile in the web of his eyes. Squeezing his eyelids tightly, he refused to let them break free. He needed to hold them back. To be strong as Sassy would want him to be. *How to be strong?* he wondered, when he was alone and alive and she was dead, lying six feet below the very dirt he stood on.

Taking a few deep breaths, he reopened his eyes, wishing things were different. Wishing she was actually here to talk to instead of a cold slab of chiseled stone. His mouth curved upward some as flashes of her smiling face treaded through his mind, reminding him that she was there, always with him. Eternally inside of him.

Ace squatted, bringing the ring from the night before out of his coat pocket. "I got this for you. I figured, what better way to display my love for you then marrying you after death. Come to think about it…" He turned his face toward the sky. "You might be the first ever to get married after death.

"Anyway, in the usual ceremonial marriage, they say the vows are broken when death *do us part*. But that's what's so special about this and us. We are unique and different from everybody else. Therefore, we must have a unique and different marriage. Nothing can tear our love apart, not even d…" Taking another deep breath, Ace fell to one knee. "Sassy, baby, I stand here now as your man, husband, best friend, and lover, and I take a vow to love you forever more, with all of me until the end of time. I promise to love you and never forget what we shared, had, and will one day have again. You are forever my life, my wife, my world."

Pausing a few moments, he imagined her directly in front of him, saying the same words. He knew deep within his heart that she was reciting them from Heaven. Letting a few more moments pass in silence, he finally uttered, "I do…" then leaned and pressed his lips against the only thing acting as a substitute for her.

"I love you, baby." His words were low yet packed with a ton of emotions. He desperately wanted to hear her return it, though he'd have to settle for confirmation within his soul.

"I'ma put this right here," Ace said as he began to part the earth with his fingers. "Don't let them grave robbers or whatever they call them muthafuckas take this. You already know I'll have any and everybody I can think of lined up, ready to dead 'em all until I find it." He let out a chuckle, knowing that her goofy self was probably saying, *"But baby, how am I going to stop them from in here?"*

"You better find a way," he muttered, covering the ring up slowly. After evening out the bulge in front of the tombstone, Ace glanced around to make sure no one had witnessed the quick burial. He wasn't surprised to see that he was the only living thing present in the cemetery. Coming to a full stand, his eyes on the last thing in life that represented his universe, he said, "I love you more."

Closing the door to the rental, Ace gazed over the distance of where he'd treaded from — a place where he wished he could remain forever. Picking up the blunt from the cup holder, he ran it under his nose. He'd been aware that it would be very necessary after leaving her gravesite. This, like everything else during these visits, was routine. He felt and tasted the blunt wrap between his lips then fired it up, taking a long, deep drag. Turning over the ignition, Aaliyah's *I Miss You* instantly resonated from the speakers as the Kush smoke exited from his lungs.

"Damn." He coughed, shaking his head slightly while removing his cell phone and pressing the power button. Turning it off when out here was his way of keeping things like they had been when Sassy was alive. Their time for only the two of them and nothing else. A couple of text messages came through seconds later. None really of much importance. Going to the call log, he highlighted the last number he'd called.

Inhaling the smoke, he waited on the other end to answer.

"Yo…" Whiteboy let out, a little groggy as if he'd been asleep.

"Man, I know yo ass ain't still in the bed, shawty?"

"Nigga, don't nobody be wit all that early shit every day."

"Ion see how when the early bird always end up with the worm," Ace said, slapping the rental in gear.

"The worm? Like who the fuck wants to eat a fucking worm?"

"Nigga, I'll eat whatever fills my stomach and pockets. Fuck you mean?!"

"Anyway…" Whiteboy yawned, releasing a deep breath, getting up. "What's good?"

"Shit, stanking mouth ass lil boy. Say though, you bout to meet Trigga in a few, right?"

"Hell yeah, what time is it?" Whiteboy asked then exclaimed after checking his phone, "Oh, shit…"

"My point exactly, nigga. Gone and handle that. The rest of them pieces, we gone put to the side, aight?"

"Bet…"

"Oh, yeah, one more thing…" Ace said, hitting the weed again. "Hit Kero and Dre them up. Tell 'em we bout to go the fuck in…"

I SEEN MY HOMEBOY DIE IN COLD BLOOD, EYES ROLL IN HIS HEAD, THERE was no love. Mama sold pussy, daddy was a fiend. We from a city where niggas don't believe in dreams... The lyrics played from the rental car's system loudly as Whiteboy pulled into QuickTrip's gas station.

Checking the scenery out, he bent slightly, adjusting the pistol on his waistline. This was common amongst damn near every nigga who ran the streets. Niggas could never be too careful in this way of life, one that continuously motivated dudes to act out their ill wills on others because of jealousy, envy, and hatred aroused by everyone's all-time favorite. Money.

"Damn…" he gasped, watching this uniquely shaped, chocolate female stroll past the car in some leggings that hugged her figure tighter than body paint, displaying every feature her bottom half offered.

Seductively, she gave him a shy grin as he turned to face her, giving her physique another thorough overlook. He could only imagine the shit he'd do to her if they ever were allowed the chance for some tete-a-tete, leisure time. He snatched open the store's door. Flirting with the store's cashier then purchasing a few items along with gas, Whiteboy walked out the same way he'd come in. Twisting the cap off the green tea, he turned the bottle upside down, swallowing a big gulp of the fluid.

Stagnant, he stood in place for another deep drink. That was when he noticed, after bringing the container downward, someone leaning against the trunk of the rental. His rental. Quickly glancing around the area suspiciously, he became certain that whoever *he* was had mistaken the rental for his very own or, most likely, someone else's. Whiteboy was definitely about to correct him. Moving closer, he observed the casualness of the big man's dress attire — all black slacks, a beige dress shirt, overlapped by a black dress coat, and a pair of black Ray-Ban shades on his face.

The guy, in Whiteboy's estimation, weighed every bit of two hundred and seventy pounds or more. He fit the description of some kind of government agent. Yet, what would twelve be doing next to the whip he was pushing? *Especially dressed the way he was in this hot ass weather?* Whiteboy had to ask himself again after taking one more glance around in an attempt to peep out an unmarked car. Then again, how was he supposed to make out one? That was the whole point of it being labeled an *unmarked car*.

Treading along the side of the vehicle, he eyed the dude closely. Reaching the rear, Whiteboy snatched open the gas tank door then slammed his soft drink on top of the car. This in no way startled the guy; he remained as he'd been over the past few moments. Then, he slowly pivoted around, displaying a smirk.

"How's it going?" offered the stranger with a foreign accent.

Whiteboy smiled. "Shid, you tell me, seeing how you all leaned up against my whip."

"Oh…" the man let out, removing his rear end from the rear end. "Well, see, I have a daughter that just absolutely love these cars, you know? It's almost like an infatuation. And you know, I'm the type of father that a just about do anything to put a smile on her face…"

Whiteboy couldn't help but to stare as if the dude was crazy. "Okay, and what does that have to do with me… and you being over here?"

"Well," the guy started out, glancing over the vehicle while clasping his hands on the top of it, "I was wondering if I could offer you anything for it?"

"Sorry, it's not for sale," Whiteboy said before waving the keys with the rectangle tag for him to see. "It's a rental."

"You sure, or are you just bluffing me?" The man's smile became broader as he tilted his shades down a bit, as if to have a better look at the car.

"I don't bluff," Whiteboy said, pulling the nozzle from the gas tank.

"Guess I can't argue with that. Now what if I inquired about another proposition?"

Whiteboy stood there, studying the man, wondering as to what this so called *proposition* would be. Maybe this would reveal the real reason he was standing here stalling him. As a reflex, Whiteboy took another careful glance around. "A proposition? I really don't do well with propositions," Whiteboy returned as he made his way to the other side of the car.

"You might want to," the man uttered, causing Whiteboy to stop in his tracks. Just as quick as the man had said it, a black SUV swerved to a halt behind him. Another reflex kicked in instantly. And Whiteboy began moving backwards with his hand feeling along his waistline. Though he thought better of it not to draw down. That would be very bad if, by chance, they ended up being some form of the police.

"Son, you might not want to do that," the man assured him, glancing down at his rumbling hand.

Hearing some kind of vehicle coming to an abrupt stop behind him, Whiteboy turned, only to see a matching black SUV a few feet from him. The back door had opened, giving him the perfect view of the guy in the backseat, who was manning an assault rifle on his lap. Deliberately aiming it at him

The fuck? Whiteboy thought, trying to analyze the predicament he was currently in. It was apparent now that these people weren't the police. They would have hopped out yelling. These muthafuckas were trying to keep whatever they were attempting to do on the hush. "What's up?" he finally spit out, fully understanding the new situation after catching sight of a dude stepping from the passenger side of the SUV behind Mr. Casual.

The big man's smile stretched wider while removing the shades from his face. "Nothing's up." He laughed, gazing upwards. "Down neither, but here, behind me, I have an associate who'd like to have a *brief* word with you," he finished, extending his arm toward the truck like a chauffeur would.

Stagnant, Whiteboy glanced around again, musing over whether it was actually possible to lessen the advantage they possessed over him at this very moment. From the looks of it, nothing within his power would aid in any way in accomplishing that. "About what?"

"Hell, I don't know. I'm just the messenger. But I'll give you my word that he won't bite. He'll have him to do that." The man laughed, looking back at the other guys who offered a smirk at the remark. "I'm just kidding but come on, kid. We don't have all day." There were no more options for Whiteboy to weigh besides the inevitable one — to find out who or what awaited him inside the SUV.

"BITCH, YO KNEES LOOK LIKE YOU BEEN PLAYING BASEBALL IN A FIELD of powder, ashy knee ass lil girl!" Ace joked on Tesha, who had been another hoodrat from around the way. A few people laughed, who had been standing around the two for the past couple of minutes as they went back-and-forth with jokes. This was the regular setting at Benny Harper's yard. Nothing going down besides drinking, smoking, gambling, some good joking, and occasionally some head busting. Music from the early eighties was always being played from the multiple twelve-inch speakers that sat on the corners of the old house. If you were within a two-block radius, you would hear the tunes clear as day.

This was the hood, his hood. Ace enjoyed sitting here, watching some of the old faces — friends and foes —interact with one another in some crazy way. He more than felt that this was where he belonged.

"Nigga, I know you ain't talking with all them low budget ass tattoos on you." Tesha cackled, glancing back at her homegirl to her left. "Talking bout that's the city tattooed on ya arm. Looks to me like you done let some child ink a bunch of club houses on your shit!" Everyone again burst into laughter.

"Bitch, you got me fucked up. Yo broke ass talking bout somebody tatts, looks like you got a portrait of Pac's morgue shot tatted on your shit!" Ace cried, dying laughing.

"Stupid ass nigga, watch ya mouth. That's my dead grandma you talking bout, bitch," Tesha snapped. Everybody was already laughing, but when Tesha stated exactly who the tattoo was supposed to be, they all cried out harder, especially Ace, who was clutching his stomach by now.

"Damn, my bad, my bad," he let out, finding it hard to be sincere and more than hard to cease his cackling.

"Boy, fuck you," sneered Tesha, walking off with a slight attitude.

After a minute, Ace leaned back against the rental, picking up his cup from the hood. He still chuckled some, along with Dre. "Man, you stupid as fuck, bra," snickered Dre before taking a sip from the Styrofoam.

"Shawty, ain even know that was her grandma. I mean, who the fuck would of thought she'd get a pic of her granny with a fuckin bandana?" Ace burst out laughing again, almost spilling his liquor.

"Man, ain't no way her gram's gangbanging," Dre chuckled. He then caught a glimpse of someone he didn't expect to see, especially not in the condition he was in. Nodding his head, he gestured for Ace to check out what had been dragging up the street. Looking worse than ever, D-nice trudged toward them. His attire was a pair of dingy ass denim jeans, with some old ass, soleless shoes on his feet, and a dirty, mechanic looking ass t-shirt. His hair hadn't been cut in weeks, his facial hair begging for attention.

Ace couldn't help but to wonder how D-nice had let himself fall off to such a low extent. Before they'd linked up, D-nice had been chasing paper. Doing him, which was the reason Ace added him to the squad. But what the fuck happened after? Where was his ambition? *No matter what happened or what the situation was, no nigga should just...* Ace began to hear those words in his head. But how could he think like that when, not long ago, he was doing the same exact thing — only in another way and for a different reason. Yet, nonetheless, the same.

Numerous times, he'd attempted to make an excuse for why he'd carried himself that way. But he had to shake them. They weren't letting him be who he was supposed to be. Plus he knew that niggas were built for anything that could take place, and if they weren't capable of handling whatever it was, then they should take heed to the aphorism by 2Pac. "If niggas can't stand the heat then stay the fuck out the kitchen."

Nothing was there for Ace to do besides drop his head due to his old protégé's current dilemma. It was one that he'd been the sole cause of — somewhat.

"What's up, Ace, Dre…" D-nice greeted, making it close to them.

"Shid, you tell us, my nigga," said Ace, trying not to sound disrespectful but a little disappointed.

D-nice owl cocked his head outwardly, not understanding where he was coming from nor where he was going with the comment. He glanced over at Dre, searching for some — rather any — type of hint. "What you mean?"

Standing erect, Ace faced him. "Shid, what's good? Why you running round these streets the way you is? Nigga, like you pose to be one of these jay muthafuckas or something. Out here looking bummy and shit. You tripping, bra."

There was nothing for D-nice to say, so in response, he hung his head low because Ace was right. How could he allow himself to tumble to such a low degree? But what else was there for him to do? He'd been kicked off the team and to the streets with nothing and nowhere to go. In all reality, he was a bum. Bums had nothing, nowhere to lay their heads, only more temporary resting spots, with nothing more to depend on besides a high that they'd waste most of their time chasing, day in and day out. And here he was, doing the exact same thing whenever the monkey rode his back, which seemed to be most of the time these days. Heroin became his sole addiction. Snatching and grabbing at his soul. Things had been all bad since he'd departed from the team and were getting worse by the day.

"Nice, man, you got to tighten up," exclaimed Dre, taking another sip, disgusted at the sight.

"What y'all niggas expect? I'm out here with nothing and nobody. Not even a place to sleep some nights so fuck it. I'm out here like the rest of these muthafuckas," D-nice spit out with pieces of saliva flying from his lips. He wondered how it was so easy for them to judge him when neither of them had walked a single day in his shoes.

Ace silently stared a moment at the nigga he'd taken out of his own home and placed within his circle, only sometime later to push him out due to his own actions. At first, he didn't feel any type of sympathy. D-nice had fucked up and lost what was all theirs on some simple minded, bird shit. At the same time though, Ace had to admit, he'd been wrong for placing all the fault on D-nice's doorstep. And for something another nigga would have done had they been in that situation!

Then, after knowing that his arch enemy, Black, had his elbow deep in it, how could he expect a person unaware of the stratagems his intellect was capable of conjuring to see what was at play and try to prevent it? It had been established in everybody's mind who stayed around Black that to be capable of outwitting any of his schemes, you'd have to possess an eagle's eye, catching every maneuver he made on niggas firsthand. This was how Ace managed to perceive mechanisms of destruction aimed at him from a mile away. Yet not just from Black but from any nigga. Black was one of the best, which gave Ace an advantage over the rest.

D-nice's words caused him to wonder as to what exactly he'd been through when he'd abandoned him. And going off his present appearance, it appeared as though he'd walked the track through hell. Ace glanced over at Dre, who was taking another swig from the Styrofoam as he looked back at them. It was like he knew he had to do something other than offer judgment.

"Say, look right," Ace started, but he was interrupted mid-sentence by an entourage of vehicles coming to a halt right across the street from them.

Keith, Ace thought, watching the slim, brown-skinned guy with a bald head, who most niggas in the hood feared and loved. Keith was an Edgewood native, who ran a few of those small streets along with his five brothers. Ace knew two of them personally due to his former boss, Black. They had made a real presence in the streets by doing the only two things that made anybody recognizable — creating lines of money like the U.S. Treasury and dropping shit off like the Nazi regime.

Their domain ran from the back of Lithonia to the last hood on the westside. And never had their established dominance been questioned.

"A bunch of smart, wild wild west ass niggas that chase the paper like death chased life…" Ace remembered the phrase Black once used to describe the pack. For a moment, Ace could have sworn he'd mistaken the direction of Keith's icy glare, yet the route he began to tread clarified all he needed to know. Instantly setting his cup down on the hood of the rental, Ace's hand fell to his pocket, tightly gripping the Glock .26 which already had one in the chamber.

Keeping one in the head was a priority whenever you were in the hood for a period of time. Any and everything was bound to happen. Better to be safe than leaking sorrily. His peripheral quickly picked up on the dudes stepping out of the vehicles, immediately following suit behind Keith, who was now only a few steps away.

"Fuck these niggas got going on?" he heard Dre utter from the back of him. He also caught wind of him tossing his cup.

"Shawty, what's up? What's all that foe?" asked Keith through his menacing smirk, acknowledging the heat in Ace's pocket.

"Nigga, you tell me?" retorted Ace, becoming ready for any sudden movement. Things would definitely pop if any such thing occurred. There was no time to play with niggas.

Keith chuckled. "Shid, nigga, I'm trying to see what's good wit that bitch who set up my muthafucking brother."

"*A bitch?* Nigga, ion know what-who the fuck you talking bout so be specific," Ace snapped, on the verge of drawing down on the entourage for even approaching him about some shit like that. Though he felt he knew exactly who he was talking about. There was nothing but one female in his world right now. And if that was who he had in mind, then he wasn't talking bout shit, period. He'd die for just thinking about *that bitch.*

"Man, fuck all this playing," growled Keith, quickly letting his hand find the item in the small part of his back.

Without hesitation, Ace's hand sprang out, about to take aim, until some nigga from Keith's rear wedged his way between the two of them.

"Bro, damn, hold fast sometimes. You tripping. All these mutha-fucking people round," the gold mouthed dude hissed, shoving Keith backwards.

"Fuck these people. What's good?" Ace's trigger finger itched to send every muthafucking person in the vicinity scattering for cover. He cared less about who saw what. None of that mattered when it came down to taking the initiative to secure his survival.

"Hold on, nigga. Don't be in a rush to disappoint yourself," snarled Gold Mouth, looking Ace up-and-down.

It didn't take a genius to get his drift. Evidently, he and Dre were outnumbered by triples, all of whose hands were out of sight, summing up the situation in case it hadn't been clear enough. Ace could take a step back and muse over the odds, but he didn't give two fucks! If this nigga, Keith, wanted it, then he'd surely deliver it to his doorstep — without the welcoming mat.

"What the fuck y'all looking at?" cursed Gold Mouth at the specta-tors who were beginning to form a small crowd around the altercation. He then, after they wasted no time in dispersing, craned his neck at the group behind. "Take bra to the whip."

"Nah," Keith protested, shoving a few of them away. "Nigga, you tripping. Ain't no way you finna try and talk this shit out wit homie, fuck nah."

"Nigga, shut the fuck up. We don't even know if he know shawty," Gold Mouth barked authoritatively, taking a swift two steps to get in his face. Without another word, Keith stared him down a moment, shot a fast glance at Ace, then proceeded in doing as told.

Ace wanted to laugh at the face he gave, as if Daddy told him he couldn't play outside with the big boys. *Some fucking killer*, he thought.

Tucking away the pistol, Ace set his eyes on Gold Mouth, who pointed aimlessly at the rear of the rental, saying, "Aye, let me holla at you ova here." Stepping sideways, Ace found it necessary to make eye contact with Dre. He knew he didn't have to utter a single word for his protégé to understand what he was thinking.

With a mere nod, Dre backpedaled toward his SUV, which was no more than a few feet away. There existed a safety measure within it which would guarantee them both leaving the way they came in case the conversation took a death spiral.

"So, what? You finna tell me what all this is about?!" questioned Ace, taking a look at the individuals lined up on the other side of the street, pretending to be an army or something.

"That's what we trying to find out. Do you know a lil brown skin chick named Ariel or Ariela? I think a nigga told me she sometimes go by the nickname Venom."

At this very moment, Ace knew he was supposed to quick draw McGraw and spray this nigga's thoughts across the pavement, especially after a swift peep told him that his comrade was in place — waiting on his cue. Gold Mouth speaking her name, along with the previous statement of the *young child,* Keith, verified exactly what he'd been thinking from the jump, and this did nothing besides aid him with an incentive to execute his first mind.

But some aspect of his mental encouraged him to stay as he was because the crux of the entire situation was about to fall from dude's lips. Yet did he really need to know? Ace did, appearing as if he was pretending to give thought about who she was. He was trying his best to keep control of himself, along with playing the bewildered role to the tee. In actuality, his brain was making an attempt to wrap around a connection between her — them and the setup brother Keith had mentioned. However, that still wouldn't get past the frustrating question of *"why the fuck is they looking for her?"*

"Nah, ion know her. So, what do all this have to do with me?" he responded, pretending to feel disrespected by the assumption.

"Shhh. Word is she run with your lil crew," Gold Mouth said, almost matter-of-factly. He eyed Ace as if he was going to get his answers from his body language.

Ace wanted to laugh. Yet he was grateful for the underestimation. The presumption would play a grave role when it finally came down to the gunplay. A misperception of your enemy most likely ended up being fatal. And this Ace understood better than most. "Really fuck a nigga word. They better have some facts cause my *lil crew,*" he emphasized, letting him know he'd read between the lines, "don't give a shit about the mishaps, the mistakes, or the mismatch. We gone do what the fuck we have to do to whoever the fuck we have to." This was his way of getting the point across that they barred none.

Gold Mouth contorted his face before smiling a little. "Shawty, all that extra aggressive shit, a nigga care less about. I'm trying to find out what happened to my brother and by who."

"Who yo brother?" Ace finally wanted to know, but he pretty much had an idea, which made its way to the forefront of his mind. Not a name but definitely a face. Now it made sense, except for the *why the fuck was they looking for her?* Or better yet, seeing how it now came together, *how in the fuck was they looking for her?*

"You probably don't know 'em, but his name Q…"

Quickly, Ace let out, "Well, I don't." Old and boring the conversation became quickly. His thinking roamed elsewhere. To be more specific, he was conjuring a few places it could have come from.

"Well, *don't* know this ho, Ariel, either, feel me?" Gold Mouth mouthed, more as a threat.

Ace couldn't help imagining planting a hollow point slug into this guy's skull. It was something that would probably transpire more sooner than later, especially if he or those other niggas were preparing to act out some revenge shit on Ariel. *No fucking way,* he said internally. These niggas — all of them — would have to be dealt with asap. But first and foremost, he needed to find out who insinuated her being involved and somehow linked her to the boy, Q. Then, somehow, linked it to him.

Ace, along with Ariel, had always made sure to keep their connection secret because, for one, he refused to let the heat fall back on her; for two, it gave an advantage to him when he needed to step on certain terrains, just not as himself. So, who'd be stupid enough to run their mouth to niggas about something they only thought they knew, unless they actually did? Almost as if God himself had spoken to him, one particular candidate came to mind.

"In due time…" Ace mumbled lowly to himself, making eye contact with Keith, who'd been coldly eyeing him down since stepping to the other side of the street. Besides him, all the other dudes, along with Gold Mouth, were muttering amongst themselves.

Keith felt he had to be the last one. "I'ma holla at you later." He smirked before stepping in the vehicle.

Ace remained silent, only offering a slight smile, seeing no logical reason in word fighting. They would for sure have a date. He glanced over at Dre, who manned the SK, in case he had to throw these dudes a surprise bloodbath. After Ace began to make his way over to him, he speedily spun back around to the alerting sound of screeching tires at the corner. Immediately, Ace's arm jerked with the gun in hand, about to level with the windshield of the vehicle, until he realized who it was. The car slid to a stop, a firearm length away from the rental he was pushing.

"What's good, bro?" Whiteboy shouted, hopping out with an AK-47 in tow. The expression displayed on his face spoke of nothing but one thing the choppa was capable of causing — havoc.

"Shit, I'ma tell you bout it. Let's pull," Ace told him, gazing over the bystanders in the yard. You could tell they wanted some shit to pop off. With everything taking place as it had, Ace had forgotten about D-nice being present. He just so happened to look toward Benny Harper's.

"Aye, Nice," he called out to D-nice, who was already looking at him. "I hope you ready to show a nigga you still got it," he finished, signaling with his head for him to take the passenger seat.

CHAPTER EIGHT

The ride was silent. Ace had cut the music off some time ago while he took in the information Whiteboy was giving. He sat there, trying to figure out who exactly the people were who had pushed up on White at the gas station.

Paul was the name of the supposed boss. Yet Ace couldn't think of one time he'd heard the name. Well, not one which belonged to some kind of mob figure. How crazy it seemed that some people had rolled up on him and basically forced him into a truck, just for Paul or whoever he was to tell him that he knew who pulled the move on the jewelry shop. He said that he didn't care to get the pieces back but instead wanted — rather needed — to have a sit down with him. Ace.

The *why* was all Ace could think about. They'd clearly made it known that it belonged to them. How they came about finding out who had it seemed perplexing. However, that part wouldn't be too hard to figure out. Hell, only four of them possessed knowledge of who was actually involved in the heist, and one had been sent to an early grave with the secret. But the other one? He'd most definitely investigate.

Damn, he almost forgot about his lil runts, who showed up afterwards. Though even with all of them in mind, it still would be a complicated task connecting any of them to the mafioso. None of them had, from what he'd seen, Mafia potential. Unless… He remembered something that appeared awkward at first yet somehow fit into the puzzle perfectly.

"What?" Whiteboy muttered, bringing the car to a halt at the red light.

"Man, that nigga, Trigga, might be trying to set us up," said Ace in a relaxed way, turning his head a little toward Whiteboy.

"Huh? You tripping. Why would shawty do some'n like that? If he wanted to set us up, bro, you don't think he could of easily pulled whatever he wanted to the other night?"

Aight, he had a point. "Okay, but what if he got us into some shit intentionally to save his own ass?"

"What? Bra, you sound crazy." Whiteboy chuckled.

"*Sound crazy!?*" mocked Ace smartly. "Nigga, did any of them folks at the gas station look like them muthafuckas we seen at the mall? The same people homie was about to squeeze on?"

Stomping on the accelerator, Whiteboy drove the car past the light, trying to bring back to mind the entire scene inside South Dekalb Mall; he found it difficult. Remembering stuff wasn't his best talent. Almost a minute later, he exclaimed, "Damn, I didn't even think bout that. But hell yeah…"

"Exactly. We need to figure out who they seeking and how we fit into the shit to make them wanna get at us," Ace told him, but he said it more to himself. He snatched the slide back on his pistol upon realizing they were only a block away from their destination.

"The guy, Paul, say he wanted to holla bout some business shit…"

"Business shit?" Ace questioned amusingly, cutting him off before he could finish. "We popped the dude's spot, and they followed you just to say, 'We need to talk some business.'"

It wasn't hard for Whiteboy to understand the point he was making, yet he still didn't believe they were up to anything dumb. To him, Paul had the perfect opportunity to take him out if that was the case. So, he could have easily dismissed that notion. But then again, what motivated them to get at them if they didn't want any of their property back? That was the real question and one he was willing to gamble on.

It wasn't every day that individuals of their caliber would pull up, wanting to add you as a tagalong. Knowing this, he realized they might be talking about big money — enough to call it real cake.

"Hit this fool," Ace told him, staring at the house they'd parked in the front of. The yard was very dark as his eyes swept over the distance of the yard. At first, Ace thought the lights were off on the inside of the house, then he remembered from the last time he visited that Tone covered the front windows with black trash bags.

Some jay shit, he thought, hearing Whiteboy say, "Say, open the door. Me and bra outside. Aight."

Impatiently, Ace swung open his door. "Nice…" he stated prior to getting out.

"Man, say no more," D-nice cut him off, hopping out of the back. The trio moved along the short walkway, cautiously watching their surroundings. They were in the hood and definitely didn't need for anybody from around the way claiming they saw such and such at such and such last. That would be an unrepairable mistake.

Whiteboy knocked on the door, and Ace watched as two jays scrolled down the block without one time glancing in their direction. Then, the sound from the locks resonated.

"What up, White? Ace…" Tone said, letting his words trail off a bit as he peeped over Ace's shoulder at the stranger who was with them. He thought he recognized him but couldn't be for sure.

"What's up, nigga? You gone let us in?" asked Whiteboy with a smirk.

"Yeah, yeah. What's good? What y'all niggas got going on?" Tone sounded a little startled as he let them in then shut the door behind them.

"Shit, really just stopping to see if you got some'n lined up." Whiteboy instantly took a nose full of the horrible smell that lingered in the atmosphere. It was the exact same stink he could have sworn he inhaled the last time.

"Nigga, you need to open a few windows in this bitch," Ace exclaimed, disgustedly fanning the air like that would help.

"Man, it don't smell that bad. Y'all just ain't used to the exquisite aroma of pussy," said Tone, staring at D-nice suspiciously.

"Yeah, dead pussy," joked Ace, making them all laugh. Without it being too noticeable, he shot a quick peek down the short hallway to see if he could catch a glimpse of whoever the junkie ho was he'd been fucking. The bathroom door was wide open and a back room door cracked.

"Man, whatever," he said, picking a half of blunt up from the ashtray. "I been on some shit. Nothing major. A couple racks."

Picking up a beer bottle from the dirty ass table, pretending to read the label, Whiteboy cut in. "Couple racks? Man, you some bullshit. A nigga starving to death waiting on you to find something. Fuck, anything!"

Ace chuckled, taking a seat at the table, which had a pile of all types of shit on it. To him, it appeared as if rodents had been lounging for years in this shit hole; *then again*, he thought, *the environment was perfect for Tone*.

"Man," began Tone, exhaling the smoke, "nigga, you act like moves just fall outta the sky or something."

Tapping his finger on the table, Ace studied his movements closely, looking for the slightest sign of nervousness. He displayed a little. But you had to know Tone to see that he was being anything besides his normal self. And Ace knew Tone, so he knew better. He'd known this nigga for years.

"Let you tell it, they do," smirked Whiteboy, giving Ace that *it's on you* gaze.

"Say, homie," D-nice began, obviously catching the same glance, "can I use your bathroom right quick? I been holding this shit dumb long," he finished, gripping the crotch of his pants.

Putting his attention on Nice, Ace wondered what the hell was on his mind because here they were, in the middle of filming a movie, and he had to pee like fuck.

Ain't no way, Ace began to think, glancing back at Tone, who said nothing at first. He only stared with suspicion, pressing the blunt back between his lips. Taking a long pull then releasing it into the air, he nodded his head, saying, "Yeah, straight down the hallway."

With a purpose, D-nice moved past Ace with a look hinting at something Ace couldn't quite grasp. However, it became clear that he had something up his sleeve. *What?* was the question.

"So, if you ain't been finding shit, what the fuck you been doing?" asked Ace, keeping his undivided attention on Tone, who moved over a little bit to watch D-nice scramble his way to the toilet.

Upon seeing the door shut behind him, Tone presumed what he was doing — inhaling another cloud of Kush, making eye contact with Ace for the first time. "Who that with y'all?" His nerves began to throb, which made Ace smile more broadly.

"A new recruit…"

"New recruit?" Tone repeated it like it had been a joke. "So what? We busting moves with bums now?" he said it more toward Whiteboy than Ace.

I'd prefer a bum over a snitch any day, Ace wanted to say, looking at Whiteboy, who still said nothing.

"Man, fuck all the suspicious shit. Nigga, what you been doing lately?" growled Ace aggressively.

Tone's expression changed to one of shock as the smoke escaped his nose and slightly parted lips. "What? What you getting at?"

"Nigga, who the fuck you been talking to?" As if on cue, Whiteboy pulled the pistol from his waistline.

Seeing the swift action, Tone began to slowly move backwards, like he was preparing to break out running. "White, what's up, bra?" he stuttered, his demeanor quickly switching to one of fear.

"Shit. Nigga, answer the question." Whiteboy locked in on him, ready for him to try some stupid shit.

"Man, shawty, I don't know what the fuck y'all talking bout. I know y'all niggas ain't saying I been talking to twelve."

"Might as well have," insisted Ace, now pulling out his gun, placing it on the table so he could have a clear view.

Tone's retinas keyed in on the pistol. "Shawty, y'all niggas hell. I ain't been talking to nobody. What the fuck I'ma…" His words were cut short by the sound of rumbling emitting from somewhere in the back of the house. Tone desperately wanted to move, so he could get a better look down the hallway, until Whiteboy gained his attention.

"Fuck nigga, don't move," he hissed, getting close up on him. Without warning, Whiteboy mushed him in the face, causing him to collide into the couch.

Ace glanced over his shoulder nonchalantly, gazing down the hall, wondering himself what D-nice had found. Probably some junkie bitch this nigga had been fucking. *Too bad for her*, Ace thought, knowing she'd share Tone's fate. The rumbling ceased. Ace stared at Tone. "Who back there?"

"Shhh, bra…" Tone shook his head.

"Nigga…" Whiteboy began but quickly paused. His eyes were transfixed on whatever was coming up the hall. Noticing Whiteboy's expression, Ace, on reflex, turned his head. "No fucking way…"

HOW THE FUCK THESE NIGGAS GONE WANT SOME BEEF SHIT? THEY DON'T even pay enough attention, Dre thought as he continued to peer through the binoculars into the night. He had been following these dudes at a careful distance for the last hour and some change, ending up on a street in some strange part of Conyers.

Picking up their trail right outside the hood, he'd expected their little duck off spot to be out of the way some. But damn, they'd made sure it was way out of the way. Every bit of an hour and a half out of the way! Closed in an upscale cul-de-sac, the house he watched them pull into the driveway of sat two houses from the end. It perfectly matched the main houses that lined both sides of the dead-end. It was dark, so he couldn't tell the exact color, though he caught sight of the only thing which made it distinguishable from the others.

There was no porch, nothing but a set of stairs running up to a door. A two-door garage set adjacent, then on the side of that was some type of small shed. Oddly built it was, which caused Dre to monitor his very own movements closely. He had run up in a lot of niggas' spots before, and a lot of times, they'd have the street pegged with watchers.

This was why he parked as far as he did. He'd definitely stick out like a sore thumb if he tried to get any closer than he already was. Nothing but a few vehicles were on the street, *probably the usuals*, he guessed, but not enough to help disguise his truck. With the binoculars up to his face, he locked on as the two people got out of the Yukon, snatched a duffle bag from the rear, then ducked up under the garage door.

Dre smiled, thinking of this little lick he'd been forced to stumble across. At first, he only wanted to locate where they laid their head since they were volunteering to be victims. But thanks to luck, he'd come to know where they laid their stash — or at least a part of it. And that was all the better.

These niggas like walking zombies, waiting — rather begging — for that one head shot, he thought, sweeping his eyes over the entire area, memorizing everything he could make out through the darkness. Difficult it was, especially with tint, so he rolled the driver's side window down to get a better look. As if this were some kind of espionage mission, he quickly made mental notes, absorbing all he could.

"Bet…" he let out moments later, feeling he'd pinpointed enough landmarks for remembrance. He was about to pull out and make a U-turn, but a car came up behind him, causing him to jerk back into the leather of his seat. He now felt the need to roll the window back up yet thought it unnecessary. Out here, in this secluded neighborhood, he was the least bit worried about someone recognizing his truck. Though a muthafucka sitting in a truck these hours of the night would draw the attention of any suspicious eyes.

The headlights protruding from the vehicle illuminated the truck's interior with a little aid from its rearview mirrors. *Damn.* Dre slouched farther into the seat, wondering why in the hell the car was taking so long to pass him. *Man, I hope this ain't twelve*, he said to himself, fighting the urge to look back. However, he knew he'd do nothing but make himself visible and very obvious on that move.

Turning his head to the side, he closely listened to the sounds coming from the car, from the motor to its tires slowly treading over the asphalt. It seemed to be creeping, something every street nigga knew could be dangerous. "Fuck they got going on?" Dre mouthed under his breath, relieved by the fact that it wasn't the police. He continued to keep his eyes on the vehicle as it slowed its way past him. It seemed like it had been creeping up until the point it had passed. Where upon right after, it picked up a little speed.

Dre stared at its taillights while it cruised farther down. Picking back up the binoculars, he peered through. The car had stopped exactly where his focus had not too long ago been. "I be damned…" he uttered loudly, not believing what he was seeing. At first, he wasn't able to make out the model of the vehicle or the individual who'd quickly exited it. The person stepped his way up toward the garage where the light from the inside sprang brightly outwards, illuminating him.

His mouth dropped while his mind spoke what he wasn't able to speak. *Ain't no fucking way.*

ACE SAT MOTIONLESS WITH MOON EYES, SHOCKED BY THE SIGHT OF what D-nice had brought from the back. He had already expected some off the wall shit dealing with Tone. However, his thoughts hadn't reached such an extent. This was some *Jerry Springer* type shit. Ace rubbed the corner of his eyes, hoping it would change the sight before him. He even closed them while doing it. But when they re-opened, D-nice was still gripping the homosexual by the back of his neck while his other arm kept control of one of the sissy's arms.

So, this how he's been occupying his time? Ace thought, glancing over at Whiteboy, whose expression spoke in multiple tones. The skin complexion on his face turned redder and redder with every moment the dude was in view. With his face resembling that of a balled-up piece of paper, Whiteboy turned to Tone. "Nigga, yo bitch ass been fucking a punk?!"

On the verge of bursting out laughing, Ace felt the need to correct his previous statement about the pussy smell. "You said dead pussy, but this nigga in here lusting over boy pussy!"

D-nice let out a lil chuckle then looked over at Tone, whose world seemed to crumble by this secret revelation being exposed. Half-naked, the sissy said nothing, only swept his eyes past Ace and Whiteboy, stopping them on Tone. They seemed to be pleading with him for help or some kind of understanding.

Feeling the strain work up his arm, D-nice pushed the punk to Tone and watched as he stupidly fell on top of him.

"Tone..." the sissy began, looking scared to death, especially after noticing the guns the two men were carrying, "please tell them I don't have..."

"Shut the fuck up," snarled Whiteboy, aiming the pistol at him.

Coming to his feet, Ace stepped closer to the two of them, presenting a menacing smile. "Now before I ask you again," was all that left his lips. Without any warning, he lifted the gun, shooting the sissy in the stomach.

"Agghh..." he coughed in pain, clutching his abdomen, unbelieving he'd really been shot... well, until the crimson began to seep through his fingers.

"Tone," Ace barked at him.

Tone stared in disbelief, eyes bulging like they were on the verge of freeing themselves from the sockets. Slowly, he turned his head toward Ace, seeing there was no other choice — unless he wanted to end up in the same predicament as his former companion.

"Now, tell me you didn't put that nigga, Keith, on point about Ariel?"

Before he had a chance to respond, the sissy called out loudly for help, begging sporadically, leading Ace to silence him, sending a bullet to his skull. The second blast startled Tone into a state of numbness. His entire body became stiff. His eyes didn't blink or anything. He just sat there, staring for a moment.

If he continued this way any longer, Ace would think his mind had made an exit with the punk's. Which would mean that his questioning was futile. This he knew, along with the fact that Ace wouldn't waste time to end his life, as he had done with his spouse.

Lips trembling, Tone began to speak cautiously and more than aware that the wrong word carried the potential of becoming his final thought. "Ace, bra, I ain't said nothing to nobody about anything. And damn sure wouldn't have told that fool, Keith," he said, holding his hands palms up, like the gesture would make it more convincing. "I mean, bra, why in the hell would I do that? That nigga, Q, was his fucking brother, and we…"

"Oh, his brother?" Ace chuckled mockingly, like he wasn't already aware of that. "Nigga," he snapped, inching closer, waiting on the slightest reason to smack the strap across his cranium, "I wouldn't of gave two fucks if it was his mama. I wanna know how he found out Ariel had some'n to do with it. Who was it — me, you, her, or White? So, is you saying that one of us told 'em?" Ace finished, pointing the pistol at him.

Shaking his head *no*, Tone looked over at Whiteboy, whose vicious stare was eating at him internally. Though he wished he'd believe him. Unable to stop it, Tone's head continued to shake. It was now obvious the situation had been a lose-lose from the start. Before Ace's inquiring, before he'd let them in, before they'd showed up. He'd known Ace for years and knew that if his mind had been made up about something, then that was just what it would be, period. But Whiteboy was present, although looking every bit of the killer he was. Yet that by itself gave him some kind of hope, even if it ran along the border of close to none. They'd formed a bond over the past few months. Robbing niggas together, busting down the spoils of their licks. Then, sometime after, they'd go out to kick shit together, just the two of them, like close friends and brothers did.

When he had first linked up with Whiteboy, he could tell that he was lacking the right hand he needed and vice versa. So it seemed inevitable that the two hook up. And slowly, but for sure, it came to pass. No, he didn't know about his connection to Ace at first, but when he found out, he warmly embraced it, not one time daring to step on his old rival's toes. Though he felt it necessary to give Whiteboy a history lesson on their relationship. Whiteboy had assured him that all would be well and not one time had he questioned it. Like close friends, Whiteboy had filled him in on the situation with Ace, one that didn't quite fit in with the Ace he remembered. Yet he couldn't see a reason for him to lie about it, crazy as it might have seemed.

And the more White vented to him about Ace's situation, the realer it appeared. And the more real it became, the more he desperately wanted to laugh, criticize, slander, yell up to God, and lastly, shake his head in pity for the once feared enforcer of the land. Damn, how things had changed. He'd thought Ace to be permanently out of the picture due to his psychological breakdown. Yet that was far from the case, especially under these current circumstances.

He'd been there for Whiteboy, so he at least expected him to return the favor somewhat or to some extent. Anything would do right now.

Tone's lips hadn't parted for close to a minute. He really didn't have a clue as to what to say. He just knew something needed to crawl from the depths of his soul, up through his esophagus, and over the small length of his tongue. Keeping his gaze on Whiteboy, he let his words escape. "Whiteboy, shawty, you… y'all know I fuck wit both of y'all…" He knew better than to exempt Ace from the equation. "I know better, and I know what's up. But on some real shit, I ain't said nothing to nobody about the shit we be doing."

Dropping his head, he stared down at his hands. It was like reality had set in, causing him to vividly see that no matter what he said or how hard he tried to convince them, his fate had been decided. Prearranged, which he came to understand was the sole reason for the third party. Lifting his head back up, he locked his eyes with Ace, the cause of it all. Staring, his mind ran over a few scenarios of how it would play out if he tried some shit. None of them ended as being a benefit to him.

Tone forced a smile to his face. "Shawty, it is what it is. Y'all gone do what y'all came to do so do it, but know I ain't never did no rat, snitch shit since my feet been planted on this earth. I'ma accept the fact that I'ma die a real nigga by a real nigga," he finished, turning his gaze toward Whiteboy now.

Ace smirked, partially amused by the brief lecture and its supposedly disrespectful ending. Neither moved him in the least way. He wanted his life, not his words. But his words for his life would be the perfect exchange.

"Real nigga…" Ace couldn't help himself. "I wouldn't say that. I would say something close to real fucking gay ass nigga."

"Or real fucking booty bandit, like they say behind the wall," Whiteboy said, wondering how in the fuck Tone's mind had come to such a sick conclusion.

Ace laughed, seeing how it irritated Tone. He paused briefly to get closer to his face, so they could be eye to eye. "On some real shit, thank you for accepting your fate… Nice." Giving the cue, D-nice whipped out the pistol Ace had given him, taking aim at his soon to be victim. He was about to squeeze the trigger until Ace stopped him.

"No, no, no. That's too quick and easy for a *real nigga*." He smiled, adding emphasis. "He got to die a privileged death." He paused, wanting to allow his words enough time to penetrate his entire existence. "Beat that nigga till he's over dead."

D-nice smiled then, without any hesitation, bounced on him, executing nothing less than what Ace desired.

CHAPTER NINE

The scenery of the Coan Park gymnasium floor was vivacious. Music blasted from the DJ's system. It was loud enough to make it seem like a concert was taking place. Tables were lined around the edge of the basketball court, catering all sorts of foods and beverages. It ranged from country fried chicken to foreign fried cuisine to all kinds of desserts, liquor of every nature, and drinks and juices of all types, courtesy of Black Lion Catering Service.

Ace and Whiteboy had financed everything with the proceeds from the jewelry lick. Which wasn't much when considering the take. They'd ate good off it — so good that Ace was intending on making the stick-up game his number one hustle. Though never would he have thought that off of one move that he'd rack in the numbers him and Whiteboy had banked by the end of it. True, at first, he'd underestimated the entire operation of the jug, along with Trigga's masterminding, and definitely the amount in which they'd gain. He couldn't see it. Hell, he'd only popped street nigga's stashes, who he knew kept bands on bands, hidden in fake secure places. It wasn't like they could just up and deposit it with the local bank without the Feds digging in their asses for the explanation of their fortunes.

But the score from Glorified Diamonds had changed his mind and life. "A residential establishment... who would of thought." Ace smiled, sweeping his eyes across the large crowd. The guests had shown up in droves. It was more than expected yet more for the better. The team, a week ago, spread word amongst the hood and a few other places close by. But man, that shit had ran through the city.

Niggas were present from damn near everywhere he could think of —_the west side, south side. There were even a few from the north side and Lithonia. Then, the females, who'd been his main objective, were even deeper. Dumb deep, outnumbering the dudes at least six to one. And by the looks of it, all of them seemed badder than a muthafucker. Easily, it could have been called *Dime Bitches Ball*.

All types of fragrances, along with the aroma of weed, treaded the atmosphere, giving it all the scents of a good time.

"Fucking right!" exclaimed Ace, glad to see that it had turned out better than he'd thought. Earlier, he left to freshen up with the impression that the party was going to be some bum shit and extra lame. However, upon returning, he quickly noticed his imagination had manifested itself into a reality. Gratefully, he moved through the crowd nonchalantly, giving a few "what's ups?" and a couple nods of the head to those familiar faces he recognized as well as to some he knew he'd never seen before. It was still all love though.

Whiteboy had told him where he'd be with the rest of the squad. Well, minus Ariel, who lamely insisted on staying in tonight out of all the nights. To him, her choice seemed very odd. Ariel, though, wasn't the party type. Hell, he couldn't remember the last time they'd been to one together. At the same time, he couldn't think of a time when she purposely missed out on one, which the team titled *SWAT*. It was an acronym they'd put together meaning Stupid Wild Ass Time. There, evidently, roamed something in her mind — something she claimed she didn't want to talk about and something he refused to let kill his vibe.

"Damn," he huffed in a whisper, coming up on a lil fine ass red bone who swayed sexily, with her apple booty, to the rhythm of the music. His retinas ran the length of her physique. Down and back up, he admired the way her dress shirt hugged tightly to every curve her body manufactured.

Catching a swift glimpse from her made it obvious she was thinking the same as he. Locking in on her face then ass, he snapped a mental picture. Surely, he'd push up and see what she was talking about without the words. Shid, judging by the look, was there a need?

Trying not to get too sidetracked, Ace remembered why he was moving and continued to pace through until finally reaching the section intended. Whiteboy, Kero, Spain, and a few more dudes from around the way were posted a few feet away on the other side of the photo set up. He licked his lips upon the sight of the beautiful females posing like models, with real bodies, for some real shots. All of them appeared to be thick in all the right places, as well as those patiently, sexily, and seductively waiting on their time in the spotlight.

Shaking his head to free himself of the photoshoot, he set his sight back on his entourage, who from what he could tell was either doing one of two things: either trying to catch a few of those females or just all out clowning them.

"Thirsty ass niggas." He chuckled to himself, hearing Whiteboy yell, "Bout time, nigga. I was starting to get lonely."

"Man, shut the fuck up." Ace laughed, dapping him up then the rest of the crew.

"Nigga, I bet you didn't think this shit would turn out like this, huh?" asked Whiteboy, waving his arm over toward the crowd before taking a sip from the liquor.

"Man, what? Ain't no way word got out like that." Ace smiled, actually appreciative the numbers had been more than expected. Yet how could he assume otherwise when free shit was up for grabs all night? What Black person in their right mind would turn down free food and liquor?

"Spain…" Ace called out, taking his attention off the weed he was about to roll up, shooting his lil homie a quick glance. "I hope this ain't no bullshit."

Tilting his head to the side, Spain gave him a look like *be for real*, saying nothing before placing his eyes back where they were.

Smiling, Ace ran his retinas over his young protégé's attire. And judging from the Polo set he was rocking, they obviously hadn't been doing too bad since he'd been off the scene though not quite like they had been before his slumber. On the other side of Spain stood Kero who, to him, seemed to be intentionally ignoring his presence. Since he first pulled up, he noticed that Kero had been the only one who hadn't said anything to him, not even a single welcoming gesture.

Ace knew he was pretending to be extra focused on the lil hos at the photoshoot. He knew Kero's interests all too well to go for something as such. Yeah, he fucked with bitches the strong way but not one time could Ace remember him being the type to sit and stare. Something was on his mind, something Ace knew had to do with him and him only. He'd previously figured that someone within the group would feel some type of way about him falling into the lil depressed state, leaving them out to dry, without intentionally doing so.

On the other hand though, he clearly understood that his slumber was only a small fraction of the problem. Very small. Niggas had love for him, true enough, but never to the point where it outweighed their love for the money.

Money. It was the one thing which made people want to ride for niggas, be their bodyguards, do boys, protégés, friends, anything they had to be. It was what people were truly loyal to. And Kero was no different. He'd been deeply in love with the money since Ace had known him, more than prepared to do whatever became necessary to put some into his pockets. Yet due to Ace's absence, his pockets had tremendously downsized — something Ace knew was the sole incentive for his feelings.

Shaking his head, he smiled. Ace wondered what would his demeanor be once he showed all of them what he and Whiteboy had put together for them to bounce back with. Hell, if Ace was right, it would, nonetheless, put them a good bit past where they'd been previously.

"Aye," he said, hitting Whiteboy to get his attention off the baby sips he'd been a little too focused on.

"What up?" asked Whiteboy, leaning toward him to hear him better.

"I'm bout to grab some'n else to drink. You want something else? Cause the way you sipping that shit seems like it's either dumb nasty or extra strong." He chuckled.

"Nah, I'm good. Ain't tryna get too lifted. Shawty, you already know the bullshit is never far from the bullshit starters."

"Nigga," began Ace, coming to his tiptoes to look over some of the crowd, "I thought that's what the fake ass security was for?"

"Rental cops. Please. What the fuck they gone stop?"

Ace knew he had a point, along with the knowledge that if any wrong shit went down, twelve would be all over this muthafucka in no time. The administrator of the property had made that very clear when he was handing him the money. "Man, just chill. Ain't nothing going down tonight," Ace assured him, heading in the direction of the liquor. He laughed, brushing by a few partiers who were dancing on the floor, executing some freaky ass moves. A bigger smile stretched across his face, thinking maybe it should have made this one of them Amsterdam, nude parties.

Finally making it through and to the other side, he quickly noticed a familiar face, one which, to his eyes, had a price tag spinning right above his head. Watching him mix up a drink for him and a bad lil female next to him, Ace crept from behind.

"Say, my nigga, you might as well mix up another one of them," said Ace, directly on dude's back. Instantly, Woo Woo became stiff, making it apparent that he'd recognized the voice. Then, he turned some to see if his assumption was accurate.

"Ace…" He smirked, sounding a little surprised. "What's up, big bra?"

"Shid, you tell me?" Ace returned halfheartedly, giving him dap and a slight embrace.

It didn't take long for Woo Woo to catch the vibe. He already knew what was on his mind. Shid, if the shoe had been on the other foot, he would have had the same shit in mind.

"Say," he said, turning back toward the female, "stay right here. Let me holla at bra right quick."

Ace and Woo Woo began to move off after hearing the girl smack her teeth, uttering, "Whatever."

With Woo Woo leading, they moved along the gym's wall until they reached the corner. "Damn, big homie, where the fuck you been?" he asked Ace, who really didn't need the small talk. He just wanted to know one thing.

"Around," he replied, glancing over the crowd before asking what he really wanted to upon the first sighting of his face. "You got that bread?"

Woo Woo's facial expression instantly changed from elatedness to that of disappointment. But who gave a fuck? Ace was standing here for his money, not an expression of hurt feelings. He just hoped for Woo Woo's sake that he had it or could locate it pronto. Because anything outside of those two would sign his death certificate.

"Ace, bra, you already know a nigga got that shit! Damn, you had to come at a nigga like that?" Woo Woo lifted his hands unbelievingly.

"I mean, I haven't heard of you trying to holla at anybody about it or get at me. So, you tell me how a nigga supposed to come at ya?" Ace studied his reaction closely, searching for a hint of deceit. There were none so far, but he couldn't help but to wonder if he possessed an extra one twenty that would definitely look good right about now.

"Man, I had told Kero a couple of times, but he was acting like you just fell off the earth or something and kept telling me to give whatever it was to him. But you gots to know I was letting nothing like that go down, especially not with that kind of paper on the line." He chuckled a little, not really noticing that Ace's attention had partially wavered off. His words had matched perfectly with the vibe Ace had felt from Kero. Though now he was beginning to think it was a little more than what he'd first thought. Something a little deeper.

No matter what the case, there was no reason for him to purposely mislead people about Ace's situation like he died or something, especially not when there was a hundred and twenty thousand at stake.

"Yeah, he hell, but when can I grab that?" Ace would figure that Kero shit out later. He wanted his paper.

"Shid, it's your money. You tell me when you want it."

Ace smiled, loving the way he made it sound. It seemed as if it had been patiently waiting on him. All of it. "That's the move. I'ma get at you in the a.m. Like early a.m. Feel me?"

"Aight, dat's what's up. Just don't be too early. You already know a nigga finna get lit then hit the telly." Woo Woo was certain he'd go in hard then give it to this ho for every bit of the remaining night.

"Say no mo. Oh, and what's ya math?" Ace quickly questioned after giving him some dap. There was no way he was about to part ways without that vital piece of info. Right now, that was a hundred twenty-thousand-dollar number.

After exchanging numbers, Ace pivoted to leave, but Woo Woo quickly halted his step. "Ace…"

Ace looked down at his hand, which was gripping his arm. This was new. He couldn't remember the last time a nigga had grabbed him like this — if a nigga had at all. His look must've displayed all that had run through his mind because just as quickly as Woo Woo had done it, he'd undone it. "My nigga, don't ever think I'd play you."

"I hope not," was all he said before walking back toward the way they came from.

Fresh drink in hand, Ace made his way back to where he'd left Whiteboy. He prayed a muthafucka didn't bump into him. Gucci Mane's *Wasted* blasted through the speakers, causing the crowd to get even more live than they already were. Every time Gucci said *wasted,* it seemed like the whole damn party adlibbed along with him.

Finally emerging from the people, Ace caught sight of his best friend occupying the exact same spot he'd left him in, nursing the same damn drink. *Automated ass nigga.* Ace chuckled at the inside joke as he approached.

"Damn, I thought you was going to the table, not the damn liquor store," Whiteboy said before taking another teaspoon sized sip from his cup.

"Nigga, if I had, I'd bet when I come back, you'd still be in the same spot with that cup…" Ace imitated his movement then laughed with him. "But anyway, I ran into that fool Woo Woo at the table."

"Woo Woo?" Whiteboy questioned, not knowing if he was supposed to remember the name or not.

"Yeah, Woo Woo. Remember shawty who I gave that work to before…" His words trailed off. He didn't want to even think about it. This most definitely was not the time or place.

Whiteboy stared a moment, trying to force it to his mind to remember. Then, as if memories saw his dilemma, it sprang to his forefront. "Oh, damn, I had forgot about that shit. Boy, what homie talking bout?!"

In that very same instant, by the look he gave, Ace could tell he'd grasped exactly what he was really saying without having to. "Shid," Ace began, letting the word drag out to give it a little suspenseful edge, "it's good!"

"That's what the fuck I'm talking about. Nigga, you the muthafucking golden child."

"Man, go head on." Ace laughed off the comment, taking a gulp from the mixed beverage.

"Real shit, bra. Things were fucked up without you. Now look, you ain't been back on the turf a full month yet, and we already running up stupid numbers," Whiteboy finished, sounding appreciative and excited.

It felt good to hear his best friend's words. To hear that things were getting back on track and was, somewhat, because of his presence. He'd been a drag session, he knew, on his comrade for too long. And just the thought of knowing it didn't end up being worthless, as it could have easily been, did a lot for him. He owed him — hell, them — and was ready to repay them all in full for never giving up on him. That was something he wouldn't be able to honestly say he'd have the patience to do. Dimples dimpled both cheeks as he peered forward where females stood in line, still waiting on their turn for glamour. Sweeping his eyes quickly around in all directions, he noticed that some, rather somebodies, were missing.

"Say, where Kero them went?" Ace wanted to know, wondering

had this been another maneuver of his young protégé in an attempt to avoid him. Yeah, now he'd have a reason to. There was no way Ace was going to let that Woo Woo situation slide. Fuck how he was feeling. That was all business, and he should have kept it solid, doing what the fuck was supposed to be done.

"Shid, ion know. They pulled right after you did. Probably seen some easy ass to snatch for tonight."

Probably, Ace thought to himself, knowing another more personal motive was at play. "Aye…" he began, getting a fast reply from Whiteboy.

"What up?"

"Did Kero ask about me?" Ace asked, aware of the answer, but he needed to check.

Lifting up one brow, Whiteboy gave him a suspicious look. "Nigga, are you being specific? Drunk? You know niggas wanna know where at all times. You top dog."

Right he was, yet he only knew about one thing he had been implying, which he hoped Whiteboy might have caught. But that wasn't the case, and this was not the time or place, he now realized. He decided to leave it there for the time being. Surely, later was a lot more attractive for every bit of his inquiring than right here right now.

"Yeah, I'm tripping. Anyway, nigga, is you gone stand here all night, toddler sipping on that watered down ass shit?" Ace snickered, playing like he was about to knock the cup from his hand.

"Hell nah! I'm really waiting on this lil ho to hit me," Whiteboy replied with a smile and another sip.

Ace grinned. "Is she real? Oh, I gots to see this bitch," he joked.

"Nigga, what? I mean, what you tryna say?"

"Nothing. Not a bitch ass thing. I just wanna see the type of bum ass hos you be fucking with. That's all."

"Bum ass hos?" Whiteboy retorted, as if even the slightest assumption of such was too disrespectful. "You got me all the way fucked up. Been had some bad lil' ones on the team," exclaimed Whiteboy confidently.

"*Team?* Man, please, what you running, some unqualified, mis-challenged, lil' league shit?" Ace tried to be reasonable. The last time he'd seen Whiteboy with anything, it was damn near a year ago. The bitch had a nice smile, but the rest of her was washed the fuck up, like one of them old sandbags people stumbled across at the beach. Most definitely out of use and out of date.

"Aight, think it's a game," uttered White, hoping — rather praying — Ace wouldn't witness the girl he'd been referencing to; he certainly laugh out of shock. But then again, it really didn't matter. Lil mama was a nice lil' ho and a dumb good fuck.

"Well, man, show me."

"Nah, how bout you show me?" Whiteboy needed a diversion.

Ace stared him up and down, wondering if he was really serious. Everybody and their mama knew there didn't exist a female he couldn't catch, even on his worst day. He'd bagged and tagged almost half the city and wouldn't hesitate one moment in finishing the rest — however many there were. "Man, chill. Don't do that." He shook his head nonchalantly with a dismissive wave of the hand.

"Nah, nigga. Show me what yo bag game like," Whiteboy insisted, knowing if he kept it going, Ace would be out his hair in no time. He smirked, putting the cup up to his lips once more.

"Aight..." Ace started out, maneuvering so they could be face-to-face. "I tell you what. We gone bet on who can snatch the baddest ho by the end of the night. And I'ma be a gentleman by letting you make it easy on yourself. Put a number on it."

Standing in place, Whiteboy silently weighed his chances of winning. This would be the foundation of his wager. Ace, he knew, had a mean way with females, quite naturally. It seemed more like a talent he possessed; he had to do nothing more than show face and smile. Likewise, he, himself, was an eye catcher of some of the baddest in the city. But in liking what he liked, or whatever you wanted to call them, he had his preference.

Though his choice of women wasn't the matter at hand. Well, it kind of was but wasn't. Money would be on the line, so his likes would be out the window. He'd have to snatch something no nigga could turn down or walk away from — a female whose skin stretched perfectly over every aspect of her physique, nicely curving over each muscle of thickness, remaining tight to bring the best in every bulge of her figure. Her face needed to define immaculate in its very own unique way. Everything about her had to scream out to the heavens *bad bitch*.

"Man, it don't take all day to do nothing," snapped Ace, bringing him back to reality.

"Nigga, I'm trying to make this shit easy on you. Hate to fall out bout a few pesos."

"Please! You acting like I'm not Ace and you not Whiteboy. Ha!" yapped Ace, along with a fake laugh.

Whiteboy twisted his lips as his eyes rolled to the ceiling. He was certain he could bag the chick of his imagination — if she existed in here tonight. But he had to ask himself if that would be enough. These types of women came by the dozens in the city, and some were even badder than them. He wasn't trying to lose no game work fucking around with Ace.

Then again, they'd popped for a dumb lil check, so he could afford it. Though what he couldn't was the bragging rights Ace would hang over his head — something he pretty much figured was on Ace's agenda, had been on Ace's agenda from the beginning.

"Two bands," mouthed Whiteboy a little arrogantly, aware of what would follow.

"Times five," spit Ace, feeling as though the bread was already in his pocket.

"Then times two." Whiteboy was hoping to bluff him, but he accomplished nothing besides the opposite.

"Oh, bet!" Ace smiled, watching his facial features closely for a sign of seriousness. He extended his hand, ready for this. But Whiteboy refused to make that finalizing grip.

"Man, two or nothing." Whiteboy's offered his final ultimatum before he began to walk off.

"Broke ass nigga, let the games begin. But say," Ace said, reaching out to stop him, "how we gone know who the winner is? Well, how we gone know I won?"

"Shid, just snapshot that pussy." Whiteboy smiled as he left.

Two hours and nine and a half drinks later, Ace found himself posted up against a wall with some bad dark-skinned chick leaning on him, who he found it very necessary to pull from the dance floor. Kesha, she said her name was, stood at a sexy height of five-five with a dazzling frame, and if memory served right, she was someone's baby mother. She had a baby doll face and a set of hazel eyes which pierced his flesh as if they were in search of his soul.

The appearance of innocence emanated from her aura, almost taming the wild animal inside of him. But she was here, at this type of party, with these types of individuals, obviously loving to indulge in these types of things — like most hood hos — and you know what they said. Birds of a feather flocked together. However, Ace wanted to think more of her, yet the setting and the vibe she gave off told him she'd be nothing more than exactly what he'd been searching for — some bad ass action to jump into for tonight.

Seductively, she brushed her ass against his crotch, swaying it from side to side. Gripping his waist, she grinned harder, wanting to feel every inch of what was in store.

"So what you finna get into tonight?" she questioned, rubbing her head up against his chin.

Sliding his hands from her waistline down to her soft, shaped abdomen, he whispered in her ear. "Shid, you tell me. I mean, it ain't like we're not leaving together."

"Oh, yeah?" She turned a bit, sounding slightly surprised. "Is this how you ask?"

He chuckled, moving back a patch of hair from her face. "Ask? Nah, I'm definitely telling you."

"Mannish, ain't we?" She swiveled, making eye contact with him.

"I'm a man, ain't I?"

"A smart ass." She giggled, running her hand down the length of that protruding rod on the inside of his jeans.

"Yup, a smart ass that was smart enough to save you from being contaminated by the losers."

"I guess... And you just got a response for everything, huh?" With that, she gripped his rock-hard manhood tightly, ready to feel it within the depths of her body.

Damn. He was ready to pull that guy out right here — right now — so she could really get a hand on things. "So what? That's your way of telling me to shut up?"

Kesha pressed her body harder against him. His hormones raced wildly through her. "No, I got other ways of doing that, boy." Her lips caressed the nape of his neck, massaging small parts of his skin, passionately sending electric waves through the cells of his body, causing his shaft to stiffen a little more.

"We'll see, girl." He almost gasped at the way she was nibbling on his neck, along with the short strokes her hands were manipulating.

"We will," she assured him, her grip tightening more.

Damn, she begging for it, he thought, staring down into her eyes, wanting badly to kiss her. He would have had he not reminded himself that they weren't too acquainted. But did that really matter? He was forced to ask himself. Many times, he'd been caught in the moment, letting his sexual nature get the best of him, leading him to indulge in the mouth-to-mouth. Shid, there were even times when a female would just finish serving him and he'd tongue her down still. But wasn't that a part of the freaky sex game, or were niggas still supposed to be too hard for the porno shit?

Fuck it, he cursed to himself, palming a handful of her soft ass as he brought her lips to his. His phallic tongue split between her delicate lips, making way to hers, erotically brushing on the moist surface until the two began to tangle and twist around each other, engaging in an ecstatic rumble. Their lips formed to the maneuverings of the other's tongue, equally giving as much pleasure as they received. Both instantaneously became lost in the moment, lost in the taste of the other's saliva.

Ace's imagination had taken him too far, leading him very close to taking the initiative of his own desire. Before he ended up executing exactly that, he needed to divert his own thoughts. Quickly and hurriedly, he removed his cell phone from his pocket to check the time — twelve-ten.

"Damn," he uttered, louder than he'd intended to.

"What?" she questioned, hands exploring under his shirt and over his rock solid abs.

"Shit, you ready to pull?" He was already imagining how her pussy would feel.

"Oh, now you wanna be nice and ask me," she teased, letting one of her hands fall back down to his crotch, giving it another hard squeeze.

"You right." His hand gripped her ass, and he spent her around to follow his lead.

Bitch think she got all the sense. Like a nigga just gonna keep going for the dumb shit she be pulling. Fuck no and definitely not with that nigga. Her stupid ass over there playing around. Ion know what she take a nigga for, but she got me all the way fucked up if she think I'ma go out bad.

He had been standing on the other side of the gymnasium watching his ex flirt, dance, and play with the nigga he'd at one time admired and would die for, someone he used to have the utmost respect for. Things had drastically changed though. Ace, in his eyes, had become something which symbolized weakness. He'd folded when they were in need of a leader. Laid down when they needed him to stand up. How could he pretend to accept or respect what Ace had done? Sacrificing everything they'd obtained for a bitch — for the sake of love, something that wasn't supposed to be a part of a street nigga's vocabulary, period. The world they were in turned by rules... better yet, street codes. And his past had clearly broken him to an unrepairable degree.

He continued staring, venomously feeling an urge to walk straight up on both of them and plant slugs in their skulls. He probably could excuse Ace, figuring he might not have known that the lil ho up on him was his ex. Then again, other reasons wouldn't. *Damn*, he was beginning to feel some type of way as he looked on, conjuring a few ways in his mental to ruin their evening. His foot raised, taking the initiative to step in their direction, until he was cut off by a female's voice.

"Damn, nigga, do a bitch gotta make an appointment for a little face time?"

He paused, immediately recognizing the voice. *Not this ho right now*, he thought then pivoted toward the direction the words had come from. Keke was a local hoodrat he'd smashed a couple of times, which he hadn't planned on doing tonight — or ever again for that matter. The last time he'd fucked her, he noticed that the cat reeked of an irritating smell. Which still didn't stop him at the time, only caused him to make a mental note to avoid the pussy at all costs in the future. He hoped she'd prepared herself for the "shawty, that shit's a dead issue," he uttered nonchalantly.

Standing on the back of her legs, with her hands on her hips, she sucked her teeth. "Mmm, so it's like that?"

"Fucking right. The fuck it pose to be like?" he snapped, shooting her a disgusted look then craned his neck, gazing back toward Ace and Kesha.

"Nigga, you act like you all that cause yo lil' broke ass done got a lil' money." It became apparent instantly that she was trying to make a scene with all the getting loud shit. "Nigga, fuck you. You ain't shit any motherfucking way," she finished, ice grilling him.

Saying nothing, he stared at her viciously, wondering if he should choke this ho out for trying to show out on him. He didn't have time for neither. Other things needed his attention, like the movement Ace and Kesha were beginning to make.

Keke was getting in the way. "Bitch, we gone catch up." He smirked menacingly then turned away. Behind him, he could hear Keke mouthing more disrespectful slurs, which he'd later make her regret. Bumping into a few people, he continued in making his way through, watching Ace and Kesha make their way beyond the gym's threshold.

Caught up in his thoughts, he failed to notice the familiar face only a few feet away from him and closing in. "The fuck!" he snarled as someone aggressively spun him around.

CHAPTER TEN

*C*ause *when you're sleep, he's reaching for your throat. Word on the street, ya reap what cha sow...* Ace rapped along with the song as he turned the rental car into the apartments. His mood was more than good. The lil female he snatched up last night, that he smashed till the morning sun, gave him some of the best morning head a nigga could receive. He'd orgasmed to the extent that his entire body had become stiff with a few small shivers here and there. Then, on top of that, making his morning super better, he met Woo Woo, grabbing that hundred and some bands he'd missed badly.

Running into him last night made him think the nigga was bullshitting. Because on some real shit, who the fuck kept bread like that for another nigga? Especially one who'd disappeared for as long as Ace had. It didn't matter if it was your closest family. The money would have been dead the minute it touched their palms.

Most definitely a hundred bands. The fuck, he thought, feeling like things were definitely starting to look back up for him.

He'd lost everything except for his very own life. Well, what was left of it. And now though, it seemed as if karma had turned in his favor as far as the material shit went. The spiritual could only be better or revived by one thing — a thing out of the question.

"I love you…" he mumbled, remembering that special part of his soul as he parked the car in front of the apartment building. Reaching over, he snatched the duffle bag from the backseat then hopped out, heading for door one-twelve.

"Club one twelve…" he joked to himself, loving every bit of the way the lumps exuding from the duffle bounced against his leg with each step he took. Knocking, he stood patiently, waiting for one of the two occupants on the other side to answer.

They probably still knocked out, he thought. How in the hell could he have forgotten his keys? "Geeking for that fucking party," he said, remembering how he'd been speeding like he'd been on X, rushing for the door.

Ace lifted his fist, about to knock a little harder, until he caught ear of a click from the top lock. "Shawty, what type shit you on?" asked Whiteboy immediately after opening the door. It was obvious he had something on his mind.

"Nigga, you act like you a nigga daddy or some'n," Ace retorted, brushing past him. Damn, wasn't he supposed to hear those words from Ariel?

"Right now, I am. What? You don't know what the fuck we pose to be doing, which…" Whiteboy paused, taking a glance down at the Cartier timepiece, "which we'll be late for in about ten minutes."

Damn, Ace thought before recalling what their agenda was for the morning. They were going to meet up with some type of Mafia figure named Paul. Well, that was what Whiteboy told him, along with that they would meet other people first who he had the slightest clue about. A question came to mind now that he'd thought about it. "Man, they ain't even said where we pose to meet them at any fucking way. You tripping." Ace scowled, thinking it was possible for the whole thing to be a set up — exactly the way he felt about it when he first heard it.

"What the fuck you think I was doing when you knocked?"

Ace smirked. "Well, nigga, have some patience. I gotta shower." Moving toward the back room, he paused midway. "And by the way, while you was getting directions, I was getting money," he finished, throwing the duffle bag forcefully at Whiteboy.

"What's this?" he quickly questioned, catching the bag in the stomach.

"Shid, a hunnid bands," Ace said, pivoting around, leaving Whiteboy with a perplexed expression.

After a few steps, he reached for his room's doorknob. Then, he heard Whiteboy yell down the hall. "You think you got all the sense."

Ace smiled at him before going into the room. *Sleeping beauty*, he thought, looking at the bed while closing the door as quietly as he could. Ariel laid there as if she was a little girl, snuggled into a pillow.

"Damn, she so spectacular," he whispered, instantly becoming aroused by the beautiful sight before his very eyes. His mouth moistened, ready to taste every part of her physique from her head to her feet. It didn't matter, long as it belonged to her.

Ace eased into the bed, dick throbbing, wondering why he'd wasted so much time with lil shawty from the party. He had a goddess laying in his domain, who would guarantee nothing less than a heavenly encounter. Pulling the cover back a little more, he slid his hand beneath while inching close to her. Her aroma was pleasant to his nose. It actually made him thankful for having such a scent to fill his bed. Making contact with her brilliant flesh, he began to massage passionately, continuing to ease closer and closer yet slower and more seductively with each inch.

He then inhaled the delicate smell of her hair. Smiling, he wished he could taste that as well. His hand cruised along Ariel's surface until curving around to the front, squeezing between flesh and her t-shirt. Her stomach possessed magnificent ripples of abdomen. *She wanna play*, he thought, knowing that there was no way possible she hadn't awakened from all this exploring and feeling, especially the nudge from his stiff rod, which pressed forcefully into her ass cheek, as if it was ready to break itself free from his jeans and rip into her insides. He loved when she was in her acting mode though. This did nothing but make him more demanding of her attention — more dominant. More than ready to exercise his full masculine puissance, his fingers threaded their way to the soft fabric of her panty line. His head brushed slightly up against hers as his hand penetrated the seam of Heaven.

"Damn," he huffed in a muffled tone, biting down harder on his lip. She'd shaved. Her soft spot was smooth as silk, making him want to caress it wildly with nothing besides tongue. The tips of his fingers creeped slowly, expecting to pierce her orifice, dying to see how wet she was. But just as quickly as his exploration began, it came to a halt.

Suddenly, she moved, snatching his paw away from her. "Nigga, where the fuck you been? Huh?" she snapped over her shoulder at him, farther dislocating them apart.

Fuck! he yelled in his head. He'd tricked himself right into her trap. Damn, he knew to expect this, but he hoped to bypass it and give makeup sex before the problem even started. Ace dropped his head to the pillows. "Man, you know how shit be." *Well, wasn't that a dumb ass line*, he said to himself right after.

"Really?" She turned to stare his stupid ass in the eyes. "And how exactly do *shit* be, nigga?"

Shit. He knew it was over with now. Hell, he now couldn't wait to break loose. He could clearly see the storm. So, retreat was his best option. "Bae, come on. You know how we rock. What? You jumping on your emotional shit now?" Unable to help himself, he brushed a hand against her, hoping she'd see how badly he wanted her and not to ruin it.

"Ace, that was how we were before…" Her words trailed off. She had to stop herself from uttering something they weren't ready for, something that had changed the way she once felt about him and would damn sure change the way he felt, period. She just didn't know if it would be for the better or worse.

Ace lifted his head a bit, curious and a little befuddled by her words. "Before… Before what?" He sat upward, staring and wondering if she was serious right now. "Now don't tell me the *fuck a nigga, no love for a nigga, cut a nigga dick off so he can swallow it* Ariel done fell for a nigga. Nah, hell nawl." He fell backwards onto the bedding, laughing like this was the most amusing shit he'd heard in a long time.

Only if you knew, Ariel thought, on the verge of shedding a tear. Though she couldn't, not in front of him. Not now. Plus, her head was only a part of the reason she was feeling the way she was. She had to remain herself until the time came. Whenever that was.

"Ha, ha. That's why yo ass on restriction," she said, trying not to break down and cry in front of him.

"*Restriction?*" Ace reiterated the word like it had been unfamiliar to his ears. Reaching down, he tried to pull her close to him, which she resisted. "Damn, that's how you do me?"

"Ace," she began, sliding from the mattress, "go clean yo dick and clear your conscious and then maybe later I'll try to think about it."

Ain't no way she feel some type of way for real. Ace sat there, thinking, while watching her climb into the sweatpants before leaving the room. He couldn't remember one time when she'd ever turned down his wooing. Yet the day had come. Ace understood now that something was definitely on her mind — something far above her heart. Ariel made that more than evident, and he could see that whatever it was, she was dead ass serious about it.

He felt an urge to press the issue, though thought better of it to let it go until she was ready to discuss it. One thing every nigga had to respect and know about a female was that they wouldn't say a single word unless they wanted to.

It felt a little awkward getting up from the bed he shared with her without them at least kicking some shit together. Well, that part was usually after they'd fucked each other, tired. But they hadn't fucked, so he was feeling a bit sour about it. Ace prayed that it wasn't the love thing. All of his had been snatched and shattered into unrepairable pieces. Smashed into little specks of lost love. He couldn't even attempt to conjure it back together in hopes of springing something new from it.

"Damn, that a be a problem," he uttered under his breath, taking another gaze at the spot Ariel had previously been in before dropping his head, thinking it would be better to just take her advice.

The steaming shower was welcoming, just not as relaxing and mind easing as it usually would be. It was nowhere near as comforting as he'd become accustomed to. Thoughts of Ariel's actions and words continued to replay within his skull, leaving him no room to ponder about anything else. Odd and weird it seemed because never had one thing occupied his mental. For the first time, his attention had been diverted away from the flood of memories of Sassy, the other feminine entity he'd loved.

"Damn, am I feeling some type of way?" he questioned himself, twisting the nozzle to cease the shower's current. How could he not? Ariel was a person he'd cared for even more. But Sassy wasn't here, so all of his feelings had been taken away, yet nonetheless there existed a feeling for her. It was hard for him to define exactly what it was. There were no words that he knew of to describe it, but he just knew something lived within him for Ariel. But was it love? No. That was an entire different field from what they were playing on. A whole nother ball game. Or was it?

In Ace's mind, he couldn't — nor wouldn't — try to allow even the smallest microscopic portion of love to enter his mind state. However, his heart was another thing. The heart was intertwined with the emotion love to the extent of being inseparable, even to the coldest muthafucka. And if any person thought they could control it, they were in for a blind surprise.

Ace felt he was definitely getting ahead of himself to assume such. But damn, why was it resembling what he'd once felt? "Hell naw!" He scoffed at his reflection, not ready to accept or entertain the thought. He had too much other shit to figure out. Closing his eyes, he mumbled the words, "I only love you," hoping that they would resonate throughout the spiritual realm until it reached her.

After getting himself together in the new abode of silence, he made his way toward the front. *Look at his greedy ass.* Ace watched Whiteboy dive into the pot sized bowl of cereal with the money he'd brought in stacked up in front of him.

"What?" Whiteboy questioned, letting specks of milk and chewed cereal exit his mouth along with the word.

"Ever heard of not talking with your mouth full?! Damn, nigga, I got to be yo daddy too." Ace smirked, taking the seat opposite of him.

"Uh, you must have forgot what happened to my last daddy?"

"Man, fuck what happened to ya last daddy. How bout that?" Ace chuckled, grabbing a stack of the crisp bills. "Nigga, you must of ironed these?"

"Thought about it but them muthafuckas came out like that. He must have had them packed like that for a lil minute," Whiteboy said before launching another spoonful down his throat.

"Really?" Ace glanced over the pile, removing another stack, examining it closely. *How odd is that?* he asked himself before tossing one back over. "I thought we were pressed for time?"

"We is. My time. But we still got an hour and some before we meet Paulie." Whiteboy wanted that to irritate him a little, get him to see that if he would've shown up a little later, their opportunity for something beneficial might have been lost. The lil mutt ho he was hugged up with last night definitely wasn't worth it.

"Nigga…" Ace snarled, throwing the other stack of money at him.

"Now you see how it feel when you be pressing niggas for no damn reason."

"Nigga, I'm the muthafucking boss of this boat. So I can do that. And plus my pressing be fo' a real reason."

"Man, what boat?" Whiteboy chuckled, looking around. "Ion see nothing but me and you sitting at this small ass table. So stop quoting 50 Cent." Stirring his spoon in the bowl, he gazed up. "Nigga, you tripping."

"Nigga, please. You know what the fuck is up, *boy*." Ace added emphasis on the last degrading word.

"Man, shut the fuck up!" Whiteboy uttered jokingly, faking like he was about to throw a stack back at him. "By the way, you know ol girl who was up on you last night?" he said in a hushed tone, remembering Ariel was in the vicinity.

"Damn, Joey Greco ass nigga. Spying on niggas and shit," he retorted back in a hushed voice. One encounter with the foreign Ariel was enough for one morning.

"Whatever. You should be grateful a nigga be concerned, especially with the way things are now. We can't trust nobody."

He was right. And Ace was grateful — more than grateful — to have someone like Whiteboy by his side. No matter what the case might have been, he always showed him that brotherly love, even when their lifestyle left no room for sentiment.

Whiteboy knew better than to wait on a mawkish response. This was him and Ace. Their actions spoke louder than words could ever. "Anyway," he continued, consuming another spoonful, "back to the lil slut bucket you chaperoned last night. You don't have a clue as to who she was, do you?"

"No," Ace stared at him curiously, "and why should I? That lil shit was going crazy for real."

Whiteboy said nothing, only gazed back, smirking, shoving down the final spoon. Obviously, he wanted to surprise him with the girl's status if, in fact, she had one.

"Okay," Ace said lowly, tiring of the suspenseful shit, "who the fuck was she?"

"Who she used to be? Or who she is now?" he asked like it was a two-fold mystery.

"Bra, I don't give a fuck which one, just tell me, nigga," Ace mouthed, ducking his head low to the table, hoping he'd spill the beans before Ariel walked in.

Whiteboy went silent and began grinning as if he was waiting on a drum roll.

Ace raised his eyebrows, then he finally said, "Man, fuck this," pushing back from the table, about to get up.

"Aight, aight..." Whiteboy quickly mouthed, turning back to glance down the hall. "Shawty was Kero's girl. Like his *girl, girl*."

"What?" Ace sounded shocked and surprised. "His girl like someone he holding down for real? Or girl like that's just a lil ho he fucking on?"

Whiteboy's smile broadened. "That's the thing. The key word is *was*. But the *was* is followed by a *he still love her and a burn a nigga bout her*."

"Noooo!" was all Ace could manage.

. . .

"Y'ALL NIGGAS PUT DOWN," SAID J-RIDER NONCHALANTLY AFTER taking on his sixth straight point.

"Drop twenty on ya right," Spain called out, ready for his well of luck to run dry. J-Rider had been messing them up on the dice since they first started shooting with the exception of him crapping out only two times. He'd already hit Spain for a little over seven hundred and had him geeking to get on the dice. So far, J-Rider had persuaded him from taking a shot on the dice. But whenever his streak came to a halt, he'd be the next shooter.

"Nah, nigga. I'm coming out to all rights, forty." J-Rider stuffed a majority of the bills into his pockets then proceeded in dropping bills to everybody who'd put money down.

"Yen said shit," snapped Spain, spinning another twenty to the pavement. Everybody that was within the inner circle began to drop money, causing J-Rider to pivot in multiple directions without fully realizing who he was betting. This was the part of the game Spain loved, along with most dice shooters. Niggas knew that if the person shooting got distracted by trying to cover all bets, trying to be greedy, one of two things would happen. Either he'd forget his point by the time he finished placing all his bets or he'd forget who he was actually betting.

And J-Rider was definitely a greedy muthafucka, who, for the most part, would forget who he betted. That was what made him sweet until he started acting exactly like now. However, he still only hit for what he could see. Spain sat there, watching the entire time, as niggas waited till he began shooting and pocketed the wages out of his sight. Hell, he had even pocketed a few tens of his own when he wasn't paying attention.

But this upset Spain's personal homeboy, Greasy, who had been there exactly for that purpose. The two had pulled schemes on all types of niggas since they'd first linked up. They'd met at a gambling house known as the Meadow, right around the way from the West End. The dice game had taken place in the back of the establishment, which allowed enough room to fit at least forty people without it becoming jam packed.

One day while there, Spain had crapped out for the fourth straight time and decided to play the sideline rather than continue to go at it hard. He couldn't concentrate; too many niggas were on his back screaming and shouting shit loud enough to burst his ears. So, he sat back on the side and watched, hoping a few dudes would lose and be on their way out the door. It was already hot as fuck, and niggas' words and curses only seemed to draw more heat.

He gazed over the scenery, letting his eyes trail from the sweaty ass people in his view, down to the growing pile of greenbacks on the concrete. It was like money was growing out of these niggas' pockets. Every time he saw a handful of money fade in to nothing, he would think it was over. But then, he'd sweep his retinas away and back, and it would be full of more greenbacks, as if this could go on for days. Unbelievable it had been to him. Never had he witnessed so much fetty being tossed around freely, like the shit was growing on trees right outside.

Spain continued to watch more attentively now as thoughts of robbing the entire place forced its way to the forefront of his mind. It had been a minute since him and Kero had some real bread on the table. Spain made a quick estimate and was certain it could have been at least a hundred racks or more in this one room. But long story cut short, he didn't stick the place up when him and Kero would have been enough to take it down, and plus, he saw something a lil sweeter.

There was a lil ugly ass dude who was slick with his mouth and a little too swift with his hands. Spain had seen him a couple of times before, milling around the spot, weaving in and out between niggas with his fake, iced out medallion of Jesus' face. That was what made Spain give him a little attention. The piece sparkled like costume jewelry, which some females liked to snatch out of the mall to match their outfits. He couldn't help but to laugh at first. You always had broke ass niggas trying to fit in and come up at dice games. Which looked exactly like he was doing here.

Every time Spain saw him with that cheap ass neck piece, he saw him with a handful of money, more money than he thought he was supposed to have, seeing as how he'd only seen him bet like two times damn near every time he was here. And never had he seen him jump on the dice himself. This made Spain suspicious. There was no way he'd been running up numbers in the game to account for the loot gripped in his palms. He had some other shit going on, and Spain was more than determined to find out what it was. So, he began to watch him closely, stepping off deeper to the side. He watched him like a hawk in the sky watched prey. His movements were quick and swift and a little too fast for any one of the gamblers to pay attention to. Their focus was too locked on the game at hand.

Within a matter of minutes, Spain had seen all he needed to. He smiled because this was about to be a new hustle with a new acquaintance. Now weeks later, here they were, busting any and every game they came into contact with.

"What's my point?" J-Rider questioned the spectators surrounding him. A few mumbles and chuckles escaped lips, but none were a number.

J-Rider asked a second time, pivoting around, glancing from face to face, until a dude to his left said, "Man, you pose to know your point, shawty."

Others laughed and confirmed the guy's statement, which did nothing but lead J-Rider to say, "Off my money then."

Instantly, niggas began to get aggressively loud, snarling shit that didn't faze J-Rider one bit. He stood there, smirking, about to pick up his money. Shid, he'd already hit good as fuck and was looking for a way to exit anyway.

"Well, fuck it…" Spain snapped, picking up his money.

"What you doing?" J-Rider asked, sticking a hand out to stop Spain.

"Nigga, getting me. You know how the game go. You'n know your point, you lose, point blank period, and I ain bout to wait all day for you to shoot."

"Man, hell nah. You tripping, bro." J-Rider held his head up then looked at everybody else who was about to do the same thing, all of them agreeing with Spain. J-Rider waved his arm, trying to conjure a way to stop them all, but it seemed as if the odds were against him, so he knew there was only one thing to do. Confront the source.

"Spain, you got a nigga fucked up," he spat, stepping closer to him while stashing the rest of the money in his back pockets.

"Nigga, what?" Spain challenged back, shuffling the money to one hand, letting the other one make its way to his waist. Quickly, niggas went to backing up. All of them already knew Spain wasn't the fighting type, never had been. But the pistol play was certainly right up his alley.

J-Rider's body became still. He'd left his strap on the floorboard of his car because there was no telling when twelve would pull up.

Spain's features became menacing as he stared J-Rider down, ready to escalate the situation. He'd love to count the bread this nigga had already won. Then a nigga screamed out, "Man, nigga, yo point four, damn."

J-Rider could breathe again. Shit was about to get real, and he wasn't prepared. He was even more grateful and glad when another told Spain to, "Let that shit go. It ain't that serious."

After another moment of staring, J-Rider turned his gaze away, reaching to pick up the dice. "Man, drop our money," he said over his shoulder to Spain as he clicked the dice together, waiting patiently on everyone.

I should dead this fuck nigga, Spain thought but decided against it. The last thing he needed was a bunch of eyewitnesses ready to rat under the pressure of the police. So, he let it go for the time being. Along with the money.

"Four way these niggas." J-Rider smiled, stepping back a little to take his shot.

"Michael Vick!" growled Spain, stomping his foot at the dice as they crashed into the wall.

Landing on eight, J-Rider glanced back at Spain. "Nigga, drop some mo…"

"You said shit." Spain immediately released three more twenties from his band.

"Every time I shoot, nigga drop," J-Rider challenged, grabbing the dice again after matching Spain's money.

"I see you trying to load up on me. I bet you don't leave wit none of this." Spain waved the money. He shot Greasy a quick look, letting him know what time it was. Surely J-Rider and a few more of these dudes were about to come up short. Spain smirked and looked on as he continued to shoot and drop bread to the pot like he'd promised. This had turned into his type of game.

Six. the dice landed on two threes. Spain released another bill then heard a female's voice shout his name. Turning, his eyes quickly met those of Lavia, who was standing a short distance out, beautiful as ever. "Hold on," he said, putting up one finger, focusing his attention back to the game. The dice landed on snake eyes.

"Drop, nigga," J-Rider snapped, a little tired as he reached into his back pocket.

"Wait, I'm good," returned Spain. His knot was getting slim.

"Nah, nigga, put down," J-Rider exclaimed, like he knew he'd put a big dent in his pocket.

"Man, shoot." Spain could see no reason to keep dropping. Better to keep it than chance these niggas winning it from him. He wasn't planning on robbing everybody.

"Spain!" he heard her yell out again, louder than she had at first, causing him to jump a little. "Man, hold on," he shouted backwards, mad that she screamed like that.

"Don't worry, shawty. I'm about to send this nigga ass to you," barked J-Rider, praying for this point.

"Nigga, please," Spain said, seeing this nigga move a little slower now. "Yo ass tired, huh?" *Damn, this nigga need to go the fuck out*, he thought to himself, wondering what the hell Lavia wanted so badly. Probably nothing, which was the usual for her. She knew not to mess with him while he was gambling. Yet here she was, shouting his name like she was his momma.

"Seven, nigga," somebody hollered as one dice came to a stop on three while the other continued to spin.

"Give this nigga Vick," screamed Spain, hoping his words would finally work in his favor. The dice ceased its movement. "Bout fucking time," Spain spit out, raking the pile of greenbacks together, exactly like everyone else was doing. They were glad to see the dice land on a four.

"Let me get off," J-Rider said, snatching more money from his pockets.

"Nigga, get off," Spain heard a few people say in unison as he straightened out the bills, walking toward Lavia.

"Oh, you gone strike and run?" asked J-Rider, beginning to look mad.

"Nah, I'm just doing what you told her." Spain smiled, continuing to move away. "I'll be back.

"And why you yelling a nigga name like that? You see I'm gambling," Spain said smartly, finally putting the money in order. He hadn't noticed the expression on her face until he got directly up on her. "What's wrong with you?"

Tears began to roll from the webs of her eyes. "Th-they found Dre…"

"Bro, I swear they doing too much extra shit now," Ace told Whiteboy, wondering what type of stunt these so-called Mafia motherfuckers were trying to pull. They had texted Whiteboy two very emphasized messages. These were the instructions on how him and Ace were to meet up with some people who would then escort them to some location. Where had been purposely left out of the text.

This instantly gave Ace a real reason to question if this was a good idea. Ace already understood the no guns part. This was like a bylaw whenever a nigga had to have a sit down with muthafuckas like these. But then they wanted them to put their phones in airplane mode once they were within a ten-mile range. Ace quickly read between the lines. They were making sure nobody could track them by their phones. No guns. No car. No location. No phone. Clearly they would be on their own by all accounts.

Perfect way for them to do what the fuck ever they wanna do to us, Ace said to himself. He grabbed Whiteboy's phone from the cupholder and read the messages two more times before replacing it. None of this was sitting right with him, and time was of the essence. They were twenty minutes out, so they needed to put their heads together and come up with a solution.

"So, what you think?" Ace finally asked, tiring of the quietness.

Whiteboy began to shake his head a little. "Shhh, this shit crazy, bra."

"Nigga, I already know that," Ace said, irritated. "Look, we got two choices. Either we turn this bitch round now, grab all our bread, rack up some artillery, and wait for the war back in case they feel some type of way bout the jewelry shit or…" Ace paused. "Or we walk out on this ledge blindfolded."

Whiteboy looked over, studying his best friend's demeanor, feeling the huge burden of making a choice for both of them. "Ace, we in this together. I can't make no choice for both of us. That's your thang, and I refuse to have it any other way, bra. So however you wanna rock out, I'm in. Always have been. Always will be."

Ace knew it was nothing less than the devoted loyalty coming from his best friend's lips. It was the same loyalty that had shown face when he'd dropped that Arab years ago. The same loyalty that made him unhesitant to welcome him into his home at his very own risk. The same loyalty that made him willing to live in the streets for the sake of a young nigga he'd known no more than a day and a half. Whiteboy had never wavered or changed one bit since then. He'd stayed true to the pact they'd made in the woods. He was the true definition of a loyalist. His statement made Ace feel grateful to have such a nigga by his side, but as well, it made him realize how ungrateful he'd been. Whiteboy had always kept Ace's interests before his own. Yet not one time had Ace attempted to place anybody's concerns above any of his, except for that of Sassy's.

But didn't Whiteboy deserve to be in that category? Didn't he deserve the same loyalty dished back? Sure, Ace had been under the impression that it was mutual. Well, until now. He had often questioned the loyalty of others, never himself though. Not until now. Loyalty, in his opinion, was wanting for your brother what you wanted for self. But didn't he make sure he always kept more than everybody else on the team? Wasn't it remaining by your nigga after he'd fucked up? But didn't he kick D-nice to the streets for something that couldn't have been prevented? Wasn't it respecting your team's views and opinions, no matter what they were? But didn't he continuously regard the ones of his team as minor notions? Wasn't it standing firm by your nigga whenever hardships arose? But didn't he turn his back on all of them after Sassy's demise?

Ace could see himself clearly now. It hadn't taken long for him to realize how his actions resembled those of a person who'd caused him so much pain. A nigga who turned him into a monster. A person who'd taken his life. A nigga who did nothing but turn Ace into him.

Ace pulled on the sun visor. He needed a good look at himself. He needed to see the person who'd killed Sassy, who had been responsible this whole time. "Damn, what's worse than a nigga who lies to himself?" Ace said, trying to laugh it off, yet he found it hard to manage.

"What?" Whiteboy wondered if he'd heard him right.

"Nothing," he quickly returned, slapping the sun visor back up. "Say, we in. We in, and that's just what it is."

Whiteboy stared after a moment, understanding what he was getting at and was more than prepared to go any distance with his brother. Powering off his phone, Whiteboy sat it on his lap. He reached, gripping the back of Ace's neck, applying a little shake. "Fuck it, we in."

Finally making it to the parking garage, Whiteboy swerved the rental into a parking space located close to the middle. Killing the engine, they both glanced around, not knowing what to expect. Whatever it was, they'd have to roll with it.

"So, bra… and this just thinking. What if they try some dumb shit, then what?"

Ace huffed as if he wanted to laugh. "What a perfect time to ask that. Ion know bout you, but ain going out like no bitch. Fuck the bullshit."

"Boy, what. Fuck Scarface. Ain letting no cowards kill me…" Whiteboy smiled, placing his phone on the dashboard, following suit behind Ace. For some reason, that phrase caused Ace to stop and stare at him. It seemed as if he'd heard him say that before. But he couldn't quite remember.

"I'm telling ya. I done dodged death too many times to let some fucking pasta heads down bad me. That a be going out like a sack," Ace said in return. He was ready for whatever they came with. Yeah, he would be without a strap. Yep, he would be outnumbered. But he would fight fearlessly.

"They probably ain't going to try shit though," uttered Whiteboy, trying to put both of their minds at ease. This was an unusual position they were putting themselves in. Never before had they walked into such a defenseless situation, willingly at that, and then with people they had no clue about. For all they knew, these people could be setting them up because of the jewelry heist. However, it wouldn't make sense if that were the case. They had already caught Whiteboy with his pants down.

Ace began to think. Their motive had to be much more than a mere conversation. Something was important to them and somehow, so were him and Whiteboy.

"Looky, looky." Whiteboy brought Ace from his daydream. Following his gaze, Ace caught sight of the van creeping its way toward them.

"We in." Ace nodded one last time, eyeing the vehicle as it crept to a halt directly behind them.

"We in," let out Whiteboy, pushing the car door open.

Ace shot his protégé a quick look across the roof of the rental. *The fuck is this*? He smirked, concentrating on the van with the balloons and smiley faces painted on the side.

Impatiently, Whiteboy yelled out, "What up?" Nothing happened.

Everything was as still as the concrete beneath their feet. No sounds were made besides the echoes of traffic coming from a distance. And then there were hums of the van's motor idling.

"What a joke," Ace mumbled, cutting his eyes from side to side. Instantly, thoughts of his gun flooded his mind. He braced himself to make a dash for it. Purposely, he'd left the car door slightly ajar, and he'd left one in the head and was grateful for the full seventeen shot clip.

"Man, fuck this," huffed Whiteboy, a bit irritated. Looking over at Ace, he reached for the door handle. That was when it got real. The van's door snatched backwards, and three masked men hurriedly jumped out, aiming automatic rifles. Their screams were gibberish, which neither of them understood.

Fuck! Ace's mind shouted as the men gestured with their weapons for them to put their hands on the roof of the vehicle. He now wondered had they made a fatal mistake. The men became still in their military uniforms. They were definitely some kind of trained militants. Ace could tell by how they took up different positions. There had been only two types of settings where he'd seen these kinds of maneuvers executed in. One was in army movies. And the other was when the S.W.A.T. team was kicking a nigga's shit in.

The passenger door on the van swung open, getting the attention of both.

"Damn," both Ace and Whiteboy mouthed silently, watching the female step out. Her height was no more than five two or three. She had the frame of a fitness trainer with toned muscles, just not enough to subtract from her unique femininity. She was cute, but you could tell she wasn't a doll.

"Who is Ace?" she asked, switching her eyes between the two of them.

"What up?" Ace lifted one hand from the car with a half wave.

She smiled then glanced at the closest militant to him. The masked individual gave her a nod and proceeded toward him, nozzle extended.

"Come, come," he insisted with a strong accent, using one hand to make him move. Ace stepped toward them, keeping his hands chest level. The dude pointed at the trunk. Ace had been through this procedure numerous times with the police, so he already knew what they had in mind. Placing hands on the trunk, the dude quickly gave the assault rifle to the female, who held it like she had experience with it.

"Nothing is sexier than a goddess with a gun," Ace said, causing the guy to use his hands roughly. Starting at his ankles, he began to frisk him, snatching rather than feeling. Ace glanced down at him, who now slid his fingers around the inside edges of his shoes. *He too deep.* Ace smirked then turned his attention back to the main attraction. His smirk quickly ceased.

The female smiled, getting closer. She lifted the rifle to his face, as if she was ready to let loose. Ace's facial expression must have been comical because she laughed, lowering the weapon. Ace returned a halfhearted laugh, figuring he shouldn't be playing with this ho in these vulnerable conditions.

Finishing what seemed to Ace as a body cavity search without the nakedness, the guy removed a zip tie from his side pocket. "Whoa, is this necessary?" Ace asked the female rather than the dude. She was obviously the one in charge.

"Isn't everything?" she said. Ace didn't understand what the hell that meant, but the way she spoke it aroused him.

After both had been zip tied, they watched as three of the militants went through the rental like they were expecting a bomb.

"This shit crazy." Ace wondered were they really being taken to a meeting or to a concentration camp.

"Man, y'all ain't got to put that shit over our heads." Whiteboy jerked his head backwards from the guy trying to place a black cloth over it.

The men laughed. "No-no, just joking," one said, smacking the side of the van. "See, no windows."

The van, in Ace's opinion, had been a smart disguise. If you were viewing it from the outside, you'd think they were delivering balloons or something for a party. No one would ever make an assumption that there was a militia with hostages in the back.

The ride had taken what seemed like forever, and it was the

roughest Ace and Whiteboy had experienced. They were sitting on steel the entire time, so they felt every bit of every bump they hit. Damn, it was taking a toll on their asses.

Now Ace knew exactly what animals felt like when being transported. The experience was horrible. He'd been in the middle of thinking about the female up front when the van slid to a stop. *Thank God!* He wanted to yell out, but Whiteboy beat him to it. The militants laughed. Ace guessed they knew the toll it took on people. They had probably gotten the same reaction every time.

Before hopping out, one of the dudes pulled out a combat knife, freeing them of their bondage.

"Fuck!" yawned Ace, stretching his arms toward the sky. *Where are we?* he asked himself, viewing the scenery before him. They were enclosed by story high buildings. The sight gave him the idea that they hadn't left the city at all. The drive had taken — in his estimation — no longer than forty to forty-five minutes. That time frame would only allow them to travel somewhere close to the city, maybe to a surrounding county. But he knew of no county which possessed buildings of this stature.

"Finished sightseeing?" the female questioned, causing both of them to face her.

"Yeah." Ace smiled. Followed by the escorts, Ace and Whiteboy entered behind her. The aroma of exotic food rushed into their nostrils. His stomach turned. Ace could only wonder how many bodies had been carried through this same hallway, out that same rear door, by these same people. The men had done nothing to shield their weapons, which told him that everyone who used this hallway knew the things that probably took place here.

Reaching a set of double doors at the end, the female turned the knob her way a little before pulling it open. "I think they'll be good boys from here?" she said, yet it was more like asking the two of them.

"Have we been bad?" Ace said, hoping that would dead any suspicion that remained. They had made it this far without any problems, and he wanted it to continue that way. However, her next words did cause another survival thought.

"No. Well, at least not yet." She winked at him then opened the door. Damn, he wanted to take that as a sign of something she might not have intended. Though this was the wrong place and time to entertain such.

Stepping out of the corridor, they had entered a lobby full of people milling about, chatting about things of concern to them. These weren't what you called the *ordinary* people. They matched the likes of business executives, people who would scream for the *God almighty!* if they had any clue of what took place behind door number one.

Ace looked at Whiteboy. His expression spoke louder than words. This was a safe zone. Close on her trail, they paced across the floor, coming to a stop in front of a pair of elevators. Ace noticed that at no point since they'd been in the lobby had their guide glanced backwards to ensure that neither of them deviated. She probably didn't care at this point. How in the hell was she going to stop them if they decided to leave? That would be a sight to see. Even if her troops were here, they wouldn't be capable of it unless they were dying to be the next up-and-coming stars on every news channel — something he seriously doubted.

He smiled, thinking, *What a wonderful hotel,* as the elevator's door separated.

"So, we did all that to wait?" exclaimed Whiteboy, wishing he had his watch to see how long they'd been sitting. Getting off on the eighteenth floor, the female had led them to room 1809 where they'd been waiting for, he'd say, close to an hour and counting.

Ace felt the same. They'd been dropped off and left without a hint of when the guy, Paul, would show up. Or anything for that matter. *Why are they keeping us on ice like this?* he had to ask himself, glancing over at Whiteboy, who stood up from the couch. "Where you bout to go?" Ace didn't want him to leave his sight.

"Nowhere. You want some'n to drink?"

"There you go, all in these people shit."

"Shid, that's they fault. They shouldn't of left us." Whiteboy pulled the refrigerator door, taking a look in. "We got water, champagne, some type of juice, Diet Coke and… champagne and water."

"Toss me some water," Ace said, stopping a short distance away from Whiteboy.

"Water?" Whiteboy gave him a side glance. "Why water when we got *Cristal*?"

"Nigga, why *Cristal* when *we* got business?" Ace said, mocking his excitement. *Ain't no way he serious.*

"Shhh, from the looks of it, we'd probably be good and sober by the time he showed up," Whiteboy told him, tossing a bottle of water over to him. As soon as he caught it, they heard a click resonate from the front door. Ace's hand quickly dropped to his waistline. It happened out of instinct. Yet it quickly reminded him of how defense-less he was.

The door opened, and two of the guys from the van, who were now dressed in suits, entered. Immediately, the one who'd tied their hands pointed to the couch. "Have a seat," he insisted strongly.

Both complied. Ace's gaze didn't leave the door though. He wanted to finally see the reason behind all of this. Then the guy walked through the threshold with a walk that spoke of real authority, like he owned the whole place. Ace could tell he was a little up in age. Salt and pepper hair accompanied the sides of his face. His face carried a bit of ruggedness that made him appear older than his years, accompa-nied by a long scar running the length of his cheek. The way his suit hugged his figure made it clear he was in shape, like he didn't need an entourage for protection.

As he made his way over to the chair across from them, Ace could almost feel the coldness of his aura. A dead coldness emanated from his eyes, sending a chill through him. He smirked, taking a seat. "Ace."

"Paul, right?" Ace responded with a little edge in his voice.

With a nod of his head, he acknowledged that he was none other. "It seems as if you don't remember me — or at least the mention of my name."

Why would *Paul* assume he would? Ace was certain that not one time had he ever come into contact with Paul or had any dealings through a third party who made mention of the name. However, something told him Paul wasn't the type to bullshit. It didn't fit with the persona he gave off. His demeanor was sedate.

"Should I?" Ace's mind had already taken a good guess at the only person he knew that was capable of having such a connection.

"You used to work for Black, no?"

Ace's guess had been confirmed, and something else sprang inside his head that fit the picture perfect. "Yeah, used to."

"Okay." Paul chuckled, slightly amused. "Do you remember the restaurant he took you to?"

"Yeah," Ace answered quickly as memories came flashing back to life of one particular dude who he never really paid any attention to, the guy he only saw once after Black had amputated the other fool.

Fuck. He now prayed that he hadn't been lured up here for some kind of revenge for stepping on his toes twice. Ace was beginning to shift a little in his seat, becoming very uncomfortable.

"Jay was his name in case you're wondering."

Ace gritted his teeth as his adrenaline heightened. This shit could get real at any moment.

Paul seemed to be pleased at his mild aggression. He needed him to be that way. This would keep him focused on everything he was about to say.

Whiteboy noticed it as well. Apparently, something was going on which he didn't know about.

"Relax some. Just not too much," Paul spoke, smoothing a wrinkle in his tie. "And if I had felt disrespected in the smallest way, I wouldn't have waited this long to execute vengeance on you or anyone else that I felt necessary to ease my hurt feelings. I'm very responsive," Paul leaned forward with a ghastly grin, "and had I not intended for it to happen, it wouldn't have."

Ace eyed him closely as he fell back into his seat, marveling at the fact that his intentions were the fate of his protégé's head coming off in that hotel room with Black playing surgeon. He was at a loss and found it hard to comprehend. Why would he use Black to do that when he possessed so many helpers who were more than willing to do just about anything for him?

Paul waved his finger, and the dude to the right of him quickly moved to the kitchen, like he'd been waiting on that specific signal.

Ace's eyes followed him, making sure he wasn't going for something crazy. And he didn't. Only the refrigerator had been within his sights.

"Ace, I don't like for people to feel uncomfortable, nor too relaxed, around me. It's bad for business because you'll never get an honest word out of them. And I'm a man of honor. I dislike advantages and disadvantages. It takes the fun out of things." Paul paused briefly, gazing at the guy standing next to Ace. "Roberto, put him and his friend here at ease."

Ace couldn't tell if what he said was a good or bad thing. Instantly, he swiveled his head, watching the guy remove a pistol from the back of him. His face tightened as the guy held out the gun to him. He flipped it upside down, letting it hang from his index finger.

The fuck? This was unexpected. There was no way he'd just brought up that gruesome past event then right after command his bodyguard to hand him a pistol. Ace stared a moment, wondering if he was serious. Though Paul affirmed it with his next words. "Take it. Take it and check the clip. Every last one of the rounds are lethal."

Ace hesitated another second then reached and gripped the steel. *What type of game is this motherfucka playing?* he thought as he proceeded in doing as instructed. He couldn't help but to ask himself, *If he is going to do this, then why did we leave ours?*

Paul nodded his head in satisfaction, as if to say, "Not bad." In that same instance, the guy next to Whiteboy did the same.

"See, I'm a man of my word." Paul smiled and twisted the top on the V8 Splash just handed to him.

"And what's the point?" Ace had to ask after hearing the sound of Whiteboy snatching the slide, sending one into the head.

His smile broadened. "Your friend is smart. But I see you are wise.

That's exactly why you are here." Paul took a deep breath, sat the juice down, then continued. "Now that everybody's okay, let's get on with the real business."

Bout time, Ace said to himself, letting his hand grip the gun tighter. He hoped his being wise wasn't his being stupid.

"I have a job for you. Well, to be more precise, I have multiple assignments for you and your buddy here. Now before we go through the *why should you work for me and you'll think about it*, let me explain to you, or rather tell you, why you are going to work for me," Paul said, unbuttoning the last few buttons on his suit coat.

This should be real good, Ace thought, seeing as how he emphasized the *you are going to work for me* part. He definitely didn't know who he was dealing with. Nobody had ever told him what he was *going to do*, except for Missy, his mother. He was a child then and had no plans on being one today. Yet he was going to be all ears until he finished or said something he didn't like. He'd gave them guns, so he should be cautious.

"Ace, first let me explain something. I've been on to you ever since you did that sloppy ass job for me. Sloppy but effective. So, I'll give you a little credit. But not to get sidetracked. I kept my eyes on you because when I first caught sight of you, I seen a thing in you that reminded me of someone from long ago. Someone I'd also lost long ago. Someone lost amongst the stars without anyone resembling even a single touch of his characteristic. Then, there he was in you! A Black boy. You was young like he was. Innocent like he was until the phantom of murder, pain, and deceit took possession of both of you. The fire of this lifestyle filled the pupils of his eyes, exactly like it had done yours.

"I could of never missed it. I — to an extent — admired you. You had potential. But Black was your handler, and I accepted that. Hell, you was his pride and joy. His number one so I left it at that. I could of stepped on his toes, more than one time, but like I said, I'm a man of honor. You don't do disrespectful things unless somebody issues it first. He had never crossed me, partly because I was the connect, as he would say. And I fed him from the long spoon that could turn deadly if need be. My morals made me let it go, though I wouldn't forget." Paul paused to take a breath and to make sure he hadn't lost Ace, which he could tell he hadn't. Ace was locked on him like a college student on a professor right before an exam.

"Then you got older, parted ways with Black, started running your own. Still I entertained the thought of bringing you on to this side. You were vicious, had a perfect sense of direction, was a leader. Though how was I to rid you of the seeds previously planted by Black? Seeds which would be detrimental to my family. Seeds capable of destroying empires. Ace, I know and understand you as I do my own fucking son, or at least I thought I did. A situation occurred involving some people. People who you can say gained both of our undivided attentions. I'll get to that in a minute, but a situation took place because of those people. And what do you do after?"

Paul became silent as his eyes rolled upward toward the ceiling. Another thought had come to mind. "Mirrors..." he said, gesturing with his hands like most people would when about to stress something. "Mirrors can show you whatever you want to see, even things you don't. Yet mirrors project the most elaborate images until the tiniest particle, let's say a rock, or whatever you want to call it, collides into it, shattering the reflection you held as truth. Now, you can try to reconstruct that beautiful image again, piece by piece, but it'll never be as it was. You can try to revive it, but there will always be cracks to distort that image, which tells you it will never be the same again. Ace, you are that mirror, glorious and fascinating at one time. Then that itty bitty rock shattered you to pieces."

Ace wanted to lash out at him because he understood exactly what he was talking about. But who was he to be sitting here giving a fucking narration about his past? About his life? He didn't know him like that to be saying anything. Yet it seemed as if he did. This infuriated him more.

Paul's eyes narrowed on him as he reached for the V8 Splash. He gulped a small sip before he began again. He knew he'd hit a nerve, which had been his intention. He wanted him mad, raging — furious.

He needed him to unleash that reckless monster inside of him. "Ace, I brought you here to give you a chance at piecing together your mirror. Even after you have taken from me multiple times and have failed my expectations thrice!" A low, deep aggression filled his voice as he emphasized with three fingers. "I still sit here, in this room right now, and offer opportunity. My words are usually short, but I felt the need to let you hear many of them, so you could understand the *why* in all this. Please don't let me down again, Ace. Do. Not. Let. Me. Down. Again. I don't give second chances or in your case, fourths."

Ace wanted to let a couple of rounds take hold of his torso. He felt every bit of the fire treading the routes of his veins. Who was Paul to sit in front of him and make choices which he couldn't turn down? Then, to top it off, threaten him about it? He'd given him a loaded gun, which he must have forgotten. However, something deep within urged him to sit, listen, and to take heed of everything that was being said. Though he really didn't want to. His hand gripped the handle tighter, finger caressing the trigger.

"Do we have a mutual understanding?" Paul could see Ace's facial expression change. He was quite amused.

Ace stared a moment, wanting to revolt and start a singalong with the pistol. But instead, a growled "yeah" escaped his lips.

"Good…" Paul smirked, not bothered in any way by his new attitude. "Now back to the people. I will not explain the basis of the connection. We will have plenty of time for that later. But for now, they are around." Paul signaled with two fingers, as if requesting something. The guy to his left untucked his shirt, bringing from under it a manila envelope, which he wasted no time in handing over.

Paul slid it across the coffee table toward Ace. His stern visage had transformed back into the one he'd entered with. Ace picked it up. "Don't thank me. Be grateful and a little appreciation wouldn't hurt."

Placing the gun on his lap, Ace removed the contents from the envelope. His heart skipped a beat as fury raced throughout every inch of his body. It didn't even take for the photo to be fully removed for him to realize who it was. His body became motionless. His mouth wordless. His mind thoughtless.

The world he knew had stopped, and no sounds were heard. Everything had faded from existence, except for him and the photo. He stared at it. Various wounds began to spread throughout it, blood spewing from each one. Not only did it run within the picture, but it was also running crimson all around him. Red, the color of death. Many nights he dreamed of finding this one person. Torturing and mutilating this person. He wanted to force a scream from this particular human being. A scream that would cause the demons in hell to quiver and shake from its horrible sound.

This individual had been the reason and had escaped his wrath. Had been unthought about but never forgotten. And now had somehow made their way back onto death's road. It was time.

"Ace," Paul called out, along with snapping his fingers, bringing him back to reality.

Blinking, Ace glanced around, stopping his gaze on the smiling Paul. The room had gotten hotter as the crimson dissolved into nothingness. Shaking his head, he couldn't help but to peer down at the picture again, which was now back in its original state. It was time to go.

"Shawty, you good?" questioned Whiteboy, giving him a worried look.

"He's okay." Paul answered for him, loving every minute of what he was witnessing. "Nothing's better than getting that one thing you've always wanted so bad that you could taste it. Regardless of how farfetched obtaining it may seem."

He was more than right in Ace's opinion. The taste had been in his mouth for over a year. "She's everything I ever wanted," snarled Ace with a devilish grin as he stood.

"Have fun and when all is well, the number will be the same. Be sure to use it," Paul said gladly.

Ace, along with Whiteboy, were about to exit before Paul called out to them. "I almost forget. The one whose name is Antwon, or better yet he goes by the nickname Trigga, I'd stay clear of him if I was either of you. He's very bad for business and has an expected fate due. Trust me. When it hits the fan, Trigga, along with everything that makes up his little world, are going to wish that God had never contemplated the thought of bringing them into existence."

Ace, nor Whiteboy, said anything in return. They just turned and headed out. Though the speaking of Trigga's name made him question *why no words about the jewelry heist?*

Fuck it, he thought, deciding that if Paul didn't make mention of it then neither would he. Plus, there was way more important shit on his agenda, like the envelope within his grasp. Making it a few steps from the room, Whiteboy touched his shoulder.

"Aye, hold up. How we pose to get back to the car?"

"Good question." Ace was so caught up in his thinking that it had slipped his mind. "Damn, go ask 'em."

Waiting, Ace took another glance at the portrait, wondering if she would keep that same smile once she saw his face. Of course not. He smiled at the thought, singing Future's *Long Time Coming*. Because it sure had.

Moments later, Whiteboy reappeared, shaking his head while giving a big grin.

"What?" Ace asked, noticing that not one escort accompanied him, which was odd.

"Man, shit!" he let out with a chuckle.

Ace stared at him awkwardly as he moved past, trying to figure out what the hell was going on. "Nigga, what they say?"

"Oh," he stopped, gazing backwards, "they said the parking garage is like two or three blocks away from here."

Ace's mouth dropped. *Un-fucking-believable.* "All that long extra driving shit earlier for a few blocks! Man, fuck them!" Ace said angrily.

"Oh, yeah, and the other thing," began Whiteboy, pressing the call button for the elevator, "they — well, Paul — said we can keep the guns."

"Oh, yeah, where they at?"

Whiteboy said nothing, just patted his waistline.

"And mine?"

"Nigga, didn't you see me pat with both hands?"

"Man, give me my shit," exclaimed Ace as the doors opened.

DURING THE RIDE, ACE POURED THE ITEMS FROM THE ENVELOPE ONTO his lap. He showed Whiteboy the photo of Stacey, who he hadn't seen before. Ace quickly read and memorized a few of the addresses she'd frequented on a regular basis. He found it hard to believe that she had been in the metro Atlanta area this entire time. But it wasn't like he'd focused unwavering attention on finding her. The ho was D.E.A., which put her out of his reach.

And Paul's reach had to be far and wide to get hold of information like this. He had gotten everything from her place of birth all the way down to the last hotel she'd slept in. All of it was transcribed in small print — very small print — compiled into forty pages with a picture. Key points or things of importance were highlighted in bright lines. This work said nothing other than professionalism, and if Ace took a guess, he'd say it had been the product of a female.

He smiled, glancing over the entire file of a Fed by the name of Sophia Williams. It was quite obvious she possessed the ability to come and go wherever necessary. So, the act of disappearing would be nothing to her.

However, previously, he had still wanted to find her. He just didn't have any clue of where to start. Many times he'd been discouraged by the question of *how in the world would he track down a fucking D.E.A. agent with nothing besides a face to go off?* A face he only saw a few times. His first action was to check the loft he'd first met her at. Yet that turned up zero besides the guy's name on the lease, who sat in prison. Then, after struggling with the Cobb County police department to retrieve his phone, it ran under a forged name.

Landing back at square one, he figured it pointless to continue his fruitless search. Deemed it stupid to even keep trying. Chasing a Fed could easily be similar to that of chasing a ghost. Both popped up unexpectedly, and both would vanish without a trace, nothing but an impression left on the mental.

This was Ace, who didn't know the first thing about catching a Fed

—_nor a ghost for that matter. And now, as odd and unusual as it may seem, he'd gained an associate who'd been an expert in that field.

"What you looking at?" Whiteboy asked curiously.

"I don't know," Ace responded, lifting his head, gazing out the window at the blue sky above. He was trying to put something together. Then, after a few more seconds, his face dropped back toward the paper. "Aight, something ain't making sense. We both know the date that shit went down in Cobb, right?"

Whiteboy nodded his head, wondering how in the world would they forget.

"Now look at this…" said Ace, placing the sheet of paper in his face. "You see that?"

"What?"

"The date." Ace felt as if he was solving a puzzle.

"Yeah." Whiteboy wanted to see where he was taking this.

"That's a year before. Now, bra, pay close attention to the high-lighted parts." Ace put another sheet up for his eyes. "That's two years before." He swapped a second sheet for a third. "And this is three years before. Notice anything?"

Whiteboy was lucky he'd told him that much because he would have missed it. "There are more colors on the first one than the last two."

"Exactly! Now this is a year and some months after the Cobb shit."

Whiteboy glanced up and down the paper, not fully catching what he was pointing out, but then he realized that this sheet of paper carried more colors than the rest of them had. "Aight?" had been the only thing he could offer with a perplexed look.

"Listen," Ace began, obviously seeing his dilemma, "I looked over all these sheets, the four I showed you. I did it like four or five times apiece. Now, on the two- and three-years' sheets, you'll see that only addresses are highlighted that change every five to six months. But on the one year before, the addresses change every three to four months. It's crazy though. If you go back and follow the counties from the three before up to the present, it seems like with every change of address, she got closer and closer to the inner city until she reached the heart of

Buckhead. So, this ho is either banked or the Feds are paying the bills. Both, I can see."

He'd lost Whiteboy, who acted as if he was following him word for word. The last thing he wanted was for Ace to have to re-explain it to him.

"Now, from about one year before on through to the present, you'll see it's not the moving stuff like in the other pages. These are point to point movements."

"Meaning?" questioned Whiteboy, wondering when he'd spill the details on how was she getting murdered and where, which mostly was his concern.

"Meaning, she did something to make Paul's people really follow her. And likewise, she knew she was being watched and that her own — the D.E.A. — couldn't save her." Ace said it like it had been told to him directly like that.

"The D.E.A. can't stop a Mafia head? How you figure?" asked Whiteboy, remembering the books he'd read where the smartest and toughest of crime figures had been crushed by the oppressive arm of the government. Only one person he could think of was capable of outwitting the law, and that had been the infamous Jackal.

"I mean, what else could explain the rapid movements toward more public spots? And nigga, what can stop us from getting at her?"

Whiteboy had to admit he'd made a good point. However, who would the Feds see posing more of a threat, two street niggas or an entire Mafia family? Well, in this day and time, probably the two street niggas, especially seeing as how the media and government officials never failed at portraying Black males as the most vicious, violent drug smuggling thugs in America. But the serial killers were white ninety-five percent of the time, and there were no Black cartels crossing the border with those bricks. This shit was definitely backwards. He wanted to laugh at the thought. "Okay, that's what's real. So, what you think?"

Ace chose his next words carefully. "Remember what Paul said. 'People who gained both of our undivided attentions.' I think she, along with her padres, fucked up, or fucked over, Paul on some big business. Which most likely led to the whole situation that ended in Cobb." Ace rubbed his chin like it was all falling into place right before his very eyes.

"I think that Paul had a heads up prior to the shit going down. And I'm willing to bet that in some kind of way, he was profiting from it. Could of been the work or anything for all I know. But I do know that some type of agreement was made between Paul, them people — and Black…" Ace gazed over the passing world as his mind treaded down memory lane.

"They clearly didn't hold up their end, so Paul decides it's time for them to meet their God. He can't send his shooters, why? Because something a lot deeper might be at stake. So, he calls us in, takes us through the what not, and test a nigga with his phrases, caring little as to spoken words but the body language he knows will reveal words unspoken. So, he lets his eyes listen. Why do you think he uttered, 'usually my words are short'? Nothing has to be heard to be understood, and likewise, nothing has to be voiced to be communicated.

"I think the Buckhead area is some sort of safe haven for Stacey or some harmful area to Paul. He fears it has the potential to get out of his hands. So, he sends us because I want revenge, and he needs whatever it is cleaned up without himself assuming any of the risk. If shit played out the wrong way, wouldn't it look more like two street thugs attacking a female for causes other than the real reason?

"Paul has to keep his hands clean at all costs. The slightest mistake or misjudgment could be fatal. And lastly, I think shawty's go…" Ace words trailed off as he glanced around the inside of the rental. A sudden thought sprang into his mind which hadn't before. Damn, how could he have slept on the strangest yet most obvious occurrence of today?

Ace now wished he hadn't exposed his thoughts so openly. Yet he was grateful he held the last most important ones in.

"What?" Whiteboy wanted to know what had come to his mind now, seeing how he so brilliantly put all that together. He just hoped he wasn't blacking out again, like he'd done in the hotel room.

"Nothing," he quickly returned as Whiteboy swerved the car into the apartments.

"What? Nigga, you was in the mi..." Ace silenced him quickly by putting his index finger up to his mouth. Whiteboy became confused and hoped for an explanation of his weird actions. But if he didn't, it wouldn't bother him.

"I think," Ace began after realizing they'd forgotten about their cell phones, which he quickly grabbed, "shawty gone love the treats I got for her."

Whiteboy was now sure that he had finally lost it. So, he didn't respond, just hurriedly hopped out of the whip.

Meeting each other at the front of the rental, Ace said, "Shawty, they bugged the car."

"What?" Whiteboy let out, astounded.

"Nigga, they bugged the car. Put sound devices in the shit to listen to our convo after leaving them," Ace spoke as if he'd been speaking to a retarded child.

"Man, you tripping. How the hell you figure that?"

"White, stop acting so fucking naïve. Nigga, you give me another reason why they would do all that searching, take us through that long ass ride, just to pull up at a hotel a few fucking streets away. The shit wasn't to be secretive or security purposes. They used all that to distract us — and they did. Why you think that long hair bitch didn't even give us a glance when we was in the lobby? We would of ran, they still would have listened." Ace scowled as they moved in front of the apartment door.

"Bra, ion know," uttered Whiteboy, a little suspicious, unlocking the door. Upon opening it, both Ace and Whiteboy immediately caught sight of Ariel sitting on the couch, crying next to Spain, who appeared to be on the verge of throwing up tears right with her.

"He gone, bra..." Spain felt the need to speak first but was barely loud enough for either of them to hear.

"What? Nigga, speak up," Ace insisted, stepping closer to Ariel, who could only stare at him, speechless.

"He gone… Dre dead." Spain was shaking now, grabbing his head like he was about to have a nervous breakdown.

"What you mean Dre dead? I just seen that nigga last night at the party," said Ace, unwilling to accept Spain's words as truth.

"Man, big bro, they found 'em. In the bathroom at the gym, stretched out," Spain iterated, looking as if the scene was playing out right before his eyes.

"Bro? What the fuck happened?" Whiteboy said, angered by the news. "I was one of the last niggas to leave. No way bro was killed in there."

"You sure?" questioned Ace, becoming frustrated, hoping somehow that he'd heard wrong or was mistaking it all. But Ariel remained silent; her sobs were too real. Spain's expression said that it was as true as it ever would be.

"Yeah, nigga," Whiteboy snarled, staring Ace up and down like he'd tried him.

Ace realized he had to be the one to calm them. Their emotions were running high, and too many sporadic emotions in one room would amount to too many problems — problems he didn't need right now. He had to be their leader.

"Say, White, grab them some'n to drink and ya self."

"Nah, I'm good," Whiteboy quickly returned, not moving to the kitchen.

"White, get something to drink, " Ace commanded, letting him see how serious he was. Whiteboy said nothing in response, just went on.

"Ariel," he called out, getting her attention for the first time. She gazed up at him. Damn, he'd never seen her look so hurt before. It made him want to make everything alright, even the shit from this morning. "Come here, Ma," he said, pulling her to him. She stood, instantly being consumed by his hug. Her cries grew louder within his embrace. He'd expected it though. It was his job to be her comforter when she needed solace. Her shoulder to cry on when the world became too much to bear.

"Shhh… I know-I know," he whispered into her ear, kissing her on the forehead, wanting to ease her pain. Every bit of it. The streets had taken everything from him, hardening his heart to the extent that his body had almost become numb to any feeling. This morning though, somehow, she had made him feel. She had revived something in him that had died with Sassy. He'd sworn not to love another female after her. Yet his heart was yearning for Ariel to fill that voided spot inside of it. This morning, he'd brushed it off as him tripping, but now with her, in his arms, up against his body, it made the inevitable undeniable. He was in love with her.

"Ariel, baby," he softly spoke, lifting her chin. Ace stared down into her beautiful eyes, wishing the circumstances were different. Wishing he could wait for a time and place other than now and here. But his heart was taking control. "Ariel… I love you. I love you," he finally let out, fighting back tears that might have fell from his eyes had the situation been other than it was.

Ariel looked at him, speechless, never thinking she'd hear those words come from Ace's mouth. Never. Yet he'd spoken them so sincerely. His eyes said it all.

"Ace, I'm in love with you — have and always will be." Nothing more needed to be said. Ace pressed his lips up against hers. Their souls ignited as their breaths danced with each other. She'd tasted the heavenly scent of the sun. He'd savored the cool celestial breeze of the moon. Their hands gave off vibrations as they clutched each other. She could feel the drums of superb masculinity; he felt the harmonic waves of femininity. Both minds depicted universal images of each other. She saw him in the light of King Jupiter, perfect in satisfying the five senses. He perceived her in the brilliance of Queen Venus, the meritorious creation of beauty and, in his case, the revival of love.

Finally ceasing their passionate kiss, Ace glanced down at her. "We got a lot of talking to do later." He hated to see the tears ebb from her eyes. "No reason to cry." He used both thumbs to remove the watery streaks from her beautiful face. Ace turned his attention to Whiteboy, who wasn't even looking at them. He stared at the carpet like he was ready to explode. Then, he fixed his gaze on Spain, who rested his head on his arms in his lap. "Spain…" he called out.

Spain's body remained in its position, like he hadn't heard him.

"Spain!" he barked louder, knowing what his young protégé was going through, but he needed answers.

"Yo…" he returned from between his legs without the slightest movement.

"Shawty, lift your head." Ace ignored the huff he'd issued coming up. At this point, they were all feeling shitty. "How you found out about Dre?" Ace hoped his source wasn't a reliable one.

Sliding his hands up then down his face, Spain looked at him. "Man, Lavia told me."

"Lavia?"

"Yeah. Ain't no need to think she's lying. I hit his people. That shit official," Spain let out, not even turning his head toward him.

"White…" Ace started out, yet before he got the chance to ask him anything, Whiteboy cut him off.

"Shawty, nobody was left in there besides a few people taking the leftovers…"

"You think one of them could have did it?" Ace needed to know exactly who they were. But he'd settle for anything now.

"Some jays? Some jays killed Dre? Man, come the fuck on." Whiteboy scowled as if that had been some embarrassing shit to even suspect. This was Dre they were talking about, not some weak ass, nobody ass nigga.

"Aight, then maybe you missed *somebodies*."

"I missed who? You think I wouldn't of seen Dre big ass wit somebody and not remember?"

"So, explain to me how the fuck he end up in the bathroom dead? Since you so fucking sure of the shit, nigga," Ace snapped, tired of the aggressive shit he was shooting at him. Grieving was one thing, but all this extra wasn't called for.

Whiteboy stared at him devilishly. "Nigga, be for real. Don't you think I would of been the first to know if bro was in there?"

"Nigga, obviously you wasn't," Ace spat, moving toward him like he was inviting a physical altercation. Immediately, he knew he was wrong. He was the one who was supposed to act off logic instead of emotions. He was the leader, no matter how difficult it was at this very moment.

Stopping short of Whiteboy, he felt Ariel's hand grip his arm. He stood there another second before turning his gaze to Spain then to Ariel. They both had unbelieving expressions on their faces. Though Whiteboy's face spoke in mutual tones, letting him know that whatever was on his mind was also on his. *I'm tripping*, Ace began to think. He felt wrong about even wanting to go there with the only person in the world who never turned on him, the person who'd always had his back since day one. Their friendship went too deep to be on the verge of fighting one another, and never had they even come close to it. Whiteboy was his nigga. His partner in crime. His brother. His ace. The only person he'd been willing to take a bullet for if there existed a choice in the matter. Ace stood there, stiff, musing over apologizing, yet he figured it better not to. There was already too much soppiness in the atmosphere.

"Say, White," he began, letting a long, deep breath flow from his mouth, "shawty, you and Spain go find out what y'all can about bro's death. I'ma head out to Tweety's."

Without another word being spoken, Whiteboy snatched the keys from the table and was just about to pull the apartment's door open until Ace stopped him. "Aye, y'all take the other rental. We don't need everybody knowing everything we got going on. And one more thing," he said, grabbing the other keys and swapping with him, "bra, I'll knock yo ass out." Ace laughed, play punching him on the chin.

Whiteboy quickly threw up his guard. "You got me fucked up." He chuckled as him and Spain departed.

Turning to Ariel, who'd remained in the exact same spot she'd stood in since leaving the couch, Ace got close up on her, wanting to taste her soul again. But he had other objectives at the forefront of his brain that were more in need of his undivided attention.

She knew it as well and wouldn't want it any other way. Ariel kissed him on the lips with a short peck, letting her hand slide down his chest as she made her way down the hallway into their bedroom. She quickly returned with a medium sized black pouch. There had been no reason to question what laid within. He'd only used it for one thing.

He was about to say something until Ariel shushed him, placing one finger up to his lips. She more than understood and needed him to focus. "I know. We got later for that. Right now, Dre needs you."

Saying nothing, Ace took the pouch and pivoted for the door. Somebody had killed one of them. So, somebody, or somebodies, had to die as well.

To Be Continued...
IN The Streetz 4
Coming soon.

REVIEW

Did you enjoy the read?
Let us know how much by leaving us a review on Amazon and
Goodreads

OTHER BOOKS BY

URBAN AINT DEAD

Tales 4rm Da Dale

The Hottest Summer Ever

Hittin' Licks For The Holidays: Atlanta

Wet Dreams On Lockdown: The Nurse

How To Publish A Book From Prison

By **Elijah R. Freeman**

Despite The Odds

By **Juhnell Morgan**

Good Girls Gone Rogue

Good Girls Gone Rouge 2

By **Manny Black**

Hittaz

Hittaz 2

Hittaz 3

Hittaz 4

Hittaz 5

Coldhearted

Coldhearted 2

By **Lou Garden Price, Sr.**

Charge It To The Game

Charge It To The Game 2

Stuck In The Trenches

Stuck In The Trenches 2

By **Huff Tha Great**

The Swipe

The Swipe 2

By **Toōla**

Melted the Heart of a Menace

Wet Dreams On Lockdown: Lieutenant Grace

By P. Wise

Merry Trapmas: Ice & Frost

By **Mia Sky**

Thug Me The Right Way

By **DiamondATL & Nai**

Atlantastan

Atlantastan 2

By **Chris Green**

IN The Streetz

IN The Streetz 2

By **Tron Hill**

Wet Dreams on Lockdown: The Male C.O

By **Tamyra Griffin**

Wet Dreams On Lockdown: The Counselor

By **Paris Iman**

Wet Dreams On Lockdown: The Warden

By **Shawnice**

Wet Dreams On Lockdown: The Captain

By **TN Jones**

BOOKS BY

URBAN AINT DEAD's C.E.O

<u>Elijah R. Freeman</u>

Triggadale

Triggadale 2

Triggadale 3

Tales 4rm Da Dale

The Hottest Summer Ever

Murda Was The Case

Murda Was The Case 2

Murda Was The Case 3

Hittin' Licks For The Holidays: Atlanta

Wet Dreams On Lockdown: The Nurse

How To Publish A Book From Prison

STAY CONNECTED

Follow
Elijah R. Freeman
On Social Media
FB: Elijah R. Freeman
IG: @the_future_of_urban_fiction